P9-CBB-741

DISCARD

BOOKS BY PHYLLIS REYNOLDS NAYLOR

Witch's Sister
Witch Water
The Witch Herself
Walking Through the Dark
How I Came to Be a Writer
How Lazy Can You Get?
Eddie, Incorporated
Shadows on the Wall

SHADOWS
ON THE
WALL

Phyllis Reynolds Naylor

SHADOWS ON THE WALL

6146

The York Trilogy
BOOK ONE

ATHENEUM   **1982**   NEW YORK

LIBRARY OF CONGRESS CATALOGING IN PUBLICATION DATA

Naylor, Phyllis Reynolds.
Shadows on the wall.

SUMMARY: While visiting York, England, a young American,
already troubled by family problems,
is assailed by strange feelings of dread whenever
he approaches some of the ancient landmarks
of the city. This is the first book of a trilogy.
[1. Space and time—Fiction. 2. England—Fiction]
I. Title.
PZ7.N24Sf   [Fic]   80-12967
ISBN 0-689-30785-3

Copyright © 1980 by Phyllis Reynolds Naylor
All rights reserved
Published simultaneously in Canada by
McClelland & Stewart, Ltd.
Manufactured by Fairfield Graphics, Inc.
Fairfield, Pennsylvania
Designed by M. M. Ahern
First Printing July 1980
Second Printing January 1982

To Jeff, the journalist,
for whom this book was born,
his own muse guiding my pen

*I would like to express my appreciation to
G. Stan Pawson, of York, England,
whose knowledge of the people and the
countryside was especially helpful.*

PROLOGUE

IN ENGLAND, in the north country, five streams come together to make the River Ouse. The Ouse, in turn, joins the Foss, and at their junction, the Romans once built a fortress which they called Eboracum. It was at Eboracum that the Ninth Legion was stationed, and there that it disappeared from all record. Later, when Eboracum was overrun by Saxons and Danes, the name changed to Eoforwic, then Jorvik, and finally York.

During the Middle Ages, a wall was built over the old stone structure that had surrounded the Roman garrison, and was expanded to circle the town. There were four

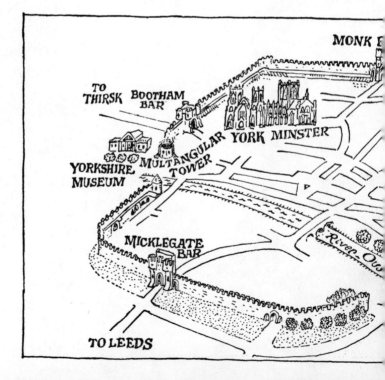

main gateways, called bars, leading into the city. Each was formed by an arch with a spiked portcullis and a heavy oak door that was shut every evening at dusk.

Bootham Bar, on the west, was actually the gateway to the north, and led through the Forest of Galtres. Armed guards were stationed at this bar to conduct travelers through the woods and protect them from wolves.

Monk Bar, on the north, commanded the road to the east, and was topped by carved grotesque figures, each holding stones. Walmgate Bar led to the southeast road and on to the Yorkshire coast.

It was Micklegate Bar through which kings and queens, coming up from the south, entered York in stately procession. But on the crest of this bar, silhouetted against the sky, the heads of traitors were exhibited on iron spikes until they rotted away, the eyes pecked out by marauding crows.

It is at this place, but in our time, that the story begins. . . .

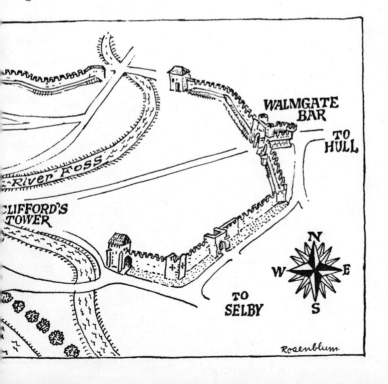

SHADOWS ON THE WALL

1

"I am whatever was, or is, or will be . . ."
—Plutarch (A.D. 46–120)

NEVER, since the world began, has a single drop of water been added to the earth, nor a single drop taken away. The cup of water in your hand may have passed through the lips of Constantine the Great or Attila the Hun. The water in which you bathe may have washed the face of hero and villain alike.

There are those who believe that some Primitive Unknown passes from spring to brook to river to sea, making all waters one, a quivering repository of collective being—that it is in the waters of the earth that life flows on, linking past to future. Some even think that, looking deep into the liquid darkness of a stream, a man can merge with all that has happened upon the face of the planet, and all that is to be.

Dan Roberts was intent upon the river. He had just crossed Lendal Bridge, leaving the Tower behind him. The uneasiness he had felt the day before gripped him again, squeezing down on his chest as he climbed the steps to the wall. He began to jog—to run, really—and the sound of his feet on the stones echoed behind him.

There was something about the river that terrified him—both the river and the Multangular Tower, secluded there in the Museum Gardens. There was something about them that spawned the fear, as though an inhuman creature was imprisoned beneath the waters or within the ancient walls of the Tower, and reached out to him as he passed. He had been in York only three days, and each morning the feeling was stronger.

He rounded the bend where the wall angled south, his throat dry, his lips parted, and thudded at last down the steps beside Micklegate Bar. Panting, he sat on a doorstep to catch his breath and wait for the terror to subside.

By the time his pulse was normal, the fear had evaporated completely. He could not understand it. Maybe it had to do with jogging—a lack of blood to the brain or something. He relaxed and leaned back against the step.

Bottles of milk, freshly delivered, stood in doorways up and down the street, the only evidence that someone was up before him. He had been going to the gate each morning because he always woke before his parents. There he would climb the steps to the ancient wall and jog around the whole town before breakfast.

He sat now, looking up at the Bar, which soared majestically above the street. It captivated him, and he found himself returning again and again during the course of a day to stare at it—absorbing the special look of its stones, the narrow slitlike windows, the banners, and the three statues that stood on the towers. The history that had been made in this place! The kings that had visited York and entered beneath this very arch, the trumpeters who had mounted the bar, the heads that had been displayed at the top. . . .

To be able to write what it was he felt when he came here, to make his words fairly shimmer with antiquity, to impart a special magic to mere black marks on white paper so that every reader would himself become a part of the past or a link to the future—that was what Dan hoped to do; to become a journalist who, when people read his writings, would say, "Of course! That's how it must have been!" or "That's how it will be, exactly."

That was some day, however—a long time off. He chafed at the years of study ahead of him—necessary, he knew—but years that separated him from what he wanted to do most: to write. He raged inwardly at times as he sat in a classroom listening to a droning lecture on predicates and participles when it was only their sound, their feel, their texture within a sentence that interested him. It was like concentrating on a leaf instead of a forest, a clock instead of the passing seasons. . . .

He was still thinking about kings and queens and traitors when he met his parents for breakfast an hour later.

"I wonder how many heads there have been, altogether, on Micklegate," he said, toying with a fish on his plate that had long since lost its eye.

"That's disgusting," said Mrs. Roberts, unfolding her napkin one corner at a time and spreading it on her lap. "Why would you want to put that in your essay when there are so many other things you could say about York?"

"It's part of the history, that's all," Dan told her.

"Just the same . . ."

There was silence again, except for the clink of forks against the china.

Dan watched his parents as they drank their tea. There was something about this trip that he definitely did not understand—something about their coming to York that seemed almost secretive. Always before, they had been able to discuss anything. Now, suddenly, any mention of death or dying or punishment or pain was taboo, as though the only acceptable topics were those that could be comfortably discussed at the table over a buttered scone. It was not like his parents at all.

Dan looked at his father. *Well, say something*, he wanted to yell. *Say anything! Don't just sit there.* He imagined the shocked faces of the waitresses in blue, who would turn toward him and stare.

But his father continued eating, his brows coming together in a thoughtful frown over the bridge of his nose. His lips barely moved as he chewed. There was nothing, it seemed, to say.

MR. STANTON'S CAB was parked outside the hotel. Both his hair and his suit were gray, though he had the face of a younger man. Even his hands had a pallid look. Whatever color there was about him came from the blueness of his eyes and the intensity of his features. It was Joe Stanton who had driven them to the hotel from the station a few days before. He remembered Dan.

"Out for a bit of a walk, are you?" He lit his pipe and leaned against the front fender as Dan came down the steps.

"Oh, just thought I'd sit here and see what goes by. You work for the hotel?"

"Not regular, you know. Train leaves for London in an hour, so I thought someone might be wanting a lift." The deep blue eyes watched a puff of smoke drift upward, then settled again on Dan. "You've been to London, I suppose?"

"Yes. We stopped there first: London, Bath, Stonehenge. But I like York better—knowing all the streets, getting around on my own. . . ."

"Your mum said you'd be staying at least a week. Chap your age must be missing a lot of school. About fifteen, are you?"

Dan nodded. "We arranged it with the principal. I get credit for the semester if I write a twenty-page essay on the history of an English city and pass a geometry test when I get back. I chose York because we're staying here the longest."

"Smart lad then, eh? The States turn out good students, do they?"

Dan smiled and shrugged. "We'll see how I do on the essay."

There was something about the conversation that was not quite right. The phrases were normal enough —questions followed by answers—but it was like two water bugs skimming the surface of a pond, never daring to penetrate the thin film, never for a moment dipping into the water beneath.

From the time Dan had first seen the man at the train station, he had felt he had seen him before— felt that if he only thought about it awhile, he would know where and when. But no memory of it came to mind: Joe Stanton was a stranger and yet not a stranger. And now, from the way the man was looking at him, Dan wondered if he felt it, too.

He was aware suddenly of the pause, the silence, and wondered if it was his turn to speak, if he had been asked a question, perhaps, that he hadn't answered. He plunged, breaking the surface tension:

"Right now I'm researching the area around the Minster. I heard about some Roman soldiers in the cellar of the Treasurer's House. Do you know any more of the story?"

Joe Stanton's eyes seemed to recede even further into his face. "Depends on how much you've heard."

"Only that someone is supposed to have seen ghosts of Roman soldiers coming through a wall or something."

"Well, there's a bit more to it than that." Mr. Stanton paused a moment with a barely perceptible reluctance, then smiled: "Not likely you'll want to put it in your essay, but about thirty years ago there was this chap, see—Martindale was the name. Can't exactly say he was a close friend of mine, but I knew him. Still around, he is. He was eighteen at the time, an apprentice plumber sent to one of the cellars to install a pipe. He was standing on a short ladder against one wall when suddenly he heard a trumpet."

The gray-haired man stopped, sucked at his pipe several times, then took a match from his pocket and relit it. Against the brightness of the flame, his hand looked almost blue.

"Well, now, it seemed most peculiar to him, his being down in the cellar like that, to hear a brass band come marching through. And then, right out of the wall where his ladder was leaning, came a Roman soldier on a horse. A large horse it was, with shaggy fetlocks. Martindale was so frightened that he fell off the ladder and scrambled into a corner. A second horseman came out, and after him more soldiers on foot, maybe a dozen or so. And they took no notice of the poor chap at all."

"This really true?" Dan asked.

"According to Martindale, and he's not a man to lie, they say. Not the first one to see them, either.

Four there were in all, at one time or another. And maybe more that aren't talking."

"What happened?"

"Nothing. The soldiers went as suddenly as they'd come. But Martindale says he saw them clearly, just as he'd see me standing here now, not looking through them at all the way they do in the picture shows."

"What did he do?"

"He was quite frazzled, you can imagine. Rushed from the cellar, collapsing at the top of the stairs, and it was there that the old curator found him. 'You've seen them, then?' says he, 'the Roman soldiers?' And Martindale knew then that it wasn't his mind playing tricks."

"Do people believe the story?"

"Well, there are those who do and those who don't. We know now, you see, that the headquarters of the Roman Legion stood on the very spot where the Minster stands. But it wasn't till a few years back, when a water main burst outside the Treasurer's House, that they unearthed the base of a Roman court. We know now that the place on the cellar wall where Martindale was leaning was the entrance to the Roman garrison."

Gooseflesh rose up on Dan's arms.

"Giving you nightmares, I suppose." Mr. Stanton smiled. "Your mum'll thank me for that." His voice was warm, reassuring and gentle. Dan decided that if he *hadn't* known him before, he was glad he knew him now.

"How about you? Do you believe in them?" Dan asked.

"Well, now, it would take either a very wise man or a very foolish one to say he didn't believe that other folks saw what they said they saw, and I don't fancy myself either one." Mr. Stanton thought it over a moment, then laughed. "Mrs. Stanton, she says she believes in ghosts because she sits across from one at the supper table every evening. Says I'm a walking apparition. With my lungs, she says, it's a wonder I can drag myself out of bed in the morning. Doctors never expected me to live as a babe, you see. And yet, fifty years later, I'm here to tell the story. Every day's a miracle. That's what almost dying will do for you."

The hotel manager, a rather plump woman, opened the door behind Dan and called down: "Two ladies are catching the nine forty-seven, Mr. Stanton. Would you drive them over?"

The man tipped his cap in answer, and Mrs. Harrison went back inside.

Dan stood up. "I'm going over to the Treasurer's House. I'll sit in the cellar for five hours if I have to and wait for the soldiers."

Mr. Stanton shook his head, and his blue eyes were darker still—like ink, deep in a bottle. "They won't let you down there, mate. You'll find them rather stuffy, I'm afraid."

Mr. Stanton was right.

"All rubbish," said the portly man in the dark suit at the reception desk. He was disappointed that Dan was not interested in paying admission to see the period furniture and artwork that adorned the upper floors. "No, we don't allow guests access to the cellars. That Martindale nonsense—that was a long time ago."

Dan went back outside, and around to the cobblestone courtyard behind, where moss grew between the pebbles. A wide black door there, only five feet high with a large iron handle, was locked. As he went back to Chapter House Street, however, he noticed a low window, without glass, at ground level. He crouched down to peer into the darkness, seeing nothing. A dank earth smell attracted him, luring him closer, but the heavy grate over the opening would not move.

Suddenly, as though unseen fingers had reached out between the openings in the grate and squeezed his heart, fear seized him again—a dread so deep, so heavy upon his chest that he gasped and reeled backward. His body was damp with perspiration, yet he trembled with cold, and he went stumbling down the sidewalk to the corner.

Once more, however, the fear disappeared as abruptly as it had begun, and he leaned weakly against a building, hands over his face. What was happening to him? What was it that made him feel so uncertain lately? What kind of cues was he getting, and from where, that made him so uneasy? Was he losing his mind?

He did not know if the sudden nameless terror came from within or without, and that, he decided, was what made it so awful. If it came from without, he could identify it, perhaps, deal with it, fight it, even. But if it came from within, his very body had turned traitor. If he couldn't trust himself, who then?

Big Peter, the deepest-toned bell in York Minster, tolled out twelve noon.

IT WAS LAUGHING TIME that afternoon. Since January, Dan had discovered, the days—and sometimes the hours within the days—had been divided between laughing times and silences. It was January when the strangeness had first begun—when his parents had started ignoring him one moment and pampering him the next, alternating between doing something fun and spontaneous and brooding darkly. It was January when they decided to go to York in the spring, decided that no other time would do, and that Dan was to come along, regardless of school.

I'm dying, he had concluded dramatically one morning, staring at himself in the mirror, his brown hair down over his eyes, lips still stained with toothpaste. *That's why all the attention, the silences. . . .*

But he had not felt as though he were dying, and there were no trips to the doctor, no questions about his throat, his lymph nodes, his head. . . . The whole thing was elusive, so vague that he could not even ask questions about it.

On this May afternoon, Dan found his parents playful. When he returned to the hotel at three, they were waiting for him. His father was loading his camera.

"Did you notice how golden everything looks

outside?" he asked. "The light's perfect. I want to get the Minster again and take more shots of the Shambles. After three days of rain, it's about time we got some good weather."

Daniel's mother was standing at the window, brushing her curly blonde hair with quick, upward strokes. "It can't possibly rain again," she said, and her voice was merry. "Mrs. Harrison said to take an umbrella with us wherever we went, but just look at that sky! This is the nicest day we've had so far."

She turned and impulsively placed her arms around her husband's neck. "Oh, Brian, we've still got a whole week left. We'll always remember this trip, won't we?"

For a brief moment Dan thought he saw the haunted look in their eyes that he'd noticed so often before, but then they were bustling about the room again, putting on shoes and jackets.

Dad's dying, Dan told himself, a thought that struck him so forcefully his stomach muscles tensed. Yet his father looked just as he always had, and there had not been any trips to the doctor for him, either. *They're divorcing,* he concluded finally. *Bill's parents divorced right after they got back from a trip to Alaska. They want something to remember. That's it.*

But that didn't seem likely either. And because he was tired of worrying about it, he put it out of his mind. He went to his own room across the hall, pulled on a sweater, and they all set out for Micklegate Bar.

Passing through the gate, they followed the curving Micklegate Street till they came to the Ouse bridge and stopped for Mr. Roberts to take a picture.

Dan leaned against the bridge and looked down into the water. A golden sheen seemed to lie like a veil over the surface. The very river up which the Vikings had sailed, and before them, the Romans! How was it, he wondered, that the fortresses they built had crumbled, the roads they laid were covered, even the land they conquered had often washed away or shifted, and yet the river remained, constant in its rush to the sea?

"Come on," Mr. Roberts was saying as he put his camera away again. "I need exercise. Let's really *move.*"

He and Dan set out, their long legs taking large swinging strides, and looked back at Mother, laughing at her because she couldn't keep up. She laughed too and waved them on, her cheeks bronze in the late afternoon sun.

Nobody's dying, nobody's divorcing, Dan told himself and felt a sudden rush of comfort.

After two blocks, Mr. Roberts stopped, laughing, and leaned against a building.

"So what are we trying to prove?" he said, his chest heaving. "Anyway we've reached the Shambles. Let's wait for Mother."

They were hungry, however, and found themselves lured into a shop redolent with the fragrance of fresh bread and spiced meats. They purchased two sausage rolls and went back outside to eat them.

"Mrs. Harrison should see us now," Dan's father said. "She doesn't believe we're ever hungry."

Dan smiled. It was true. Ever since their first meal in her hotel dining room, she had urged the waitresses to bring a little more of this or that to the Roberts' table. It was Mrs. Harrison who hovered over them at dessert time with a pitcher of thick cream and poured it lavishly over whatever they had ordered—apple pie, cheese cake—it made no difference; it was drowned in a bath of cream.

"Skin and bones!" she'd said just that morning, clucking over Dan, as she held the silver pitcher above his porridge. "What kind of cream do they 'ave in Pennsylvania?" she had asked. "What kind of cows, eh?"

"Skinny ones," Dan had said, and they'd all laughed aloud. That was before he had mentioned the heads on Micklegate Bar, bringing on the awful silence. He would have to be more careful.

"I smell sausage!" Mother said now when she caught up with them.

"Decided to fatten ourselves up before Mrs. Harrison sees us again," Mr. Roberts said. He put one arm around Dan's shoulder as they started down the narrow street whose ancient buildings on either side leaned toward each other. "We come from a long line of lanky people, Dan. Dad was tall and thin, his brother, too, and all their children. Not a stout one in the bunch. You take after me . . ."

There was something about the way his voice

trailed off and his jaw congealed over the words that
rekindled Dan's suspicions. And because he was feeling so close to his father, he took a chance:

"Dad, you're not sick, are you?"

Mrs. Roberts, who was walking ahead this time,
turned sharply. "Of course he's not sick, Dan!"

"Why?" questioned his father. "Do I act sick?
What made you ask that?"

He's sick, Dan thought, and the foreboding filled
his chest, almost suffocating him. "Just wondered,"
he said finally. "Sometimes everybody seems so secretive."

A clock in an apothecary's shop said three
twenty-one. Laughing time was over.

THEY ATE DINNER that evening in the Jorwik Room of
the Viking Hotel ("We'll splurge," Mrs. Roberts said)
and lingered long over the fruit and cheese that
ended the meal.

"Are you keeping up your notebook?" Dan's father asked him. "Not planning on writing the whole
essay after we get home, are you?"

"No, I write a little at a time." Dan looked across
the table at his mother. "How's *your* research coming?"

"I've just started checking the baptismal records
at St. Martin's Church," she told him. "I couldn't find
anything at All Saints'."

Dan sat waiting for his parents to finish their
meal, trying to piece things together in his mind. The

reason for the trip, his mother had told him, was to research his father's family tree. They had always been interested in genealogy, she'd said, but had never known much about his relatives until they'd heard from his cousin a few months ago.

"Why Dad's family and not yours?" Dan had asked, since she seemed to be doing all the work.

"Because I don't know a thing about mine. Nobody kept any records at all," she had answered. "Some day, you may be interested in genealogy yourself, and at least you'll have your father's side to start with."

That still hadn't explained it. It hadn't explained why the idea had come up so suddenly, why he had been taken out of school to make the trip. It hadn't explained why they were willing to spend so much money on this vacation—at least half their savings. It hadn't explained the strange bouts of laughing and closeness, either, followed by the silence.

"It just seemed to make sense," Mother had said when he'd pressed her about it. "We can get cheaper rates if we go before June, and I'll be taking two courses at the University this summer, so we wouldn't be able to go then. We just felt—your father and I— that if we put it off any longer, maybe we'd never get around to going. A few more years and you'll be in college anyway, so we just threw caution to the winds and bought the tickets. It's our one chance, so we might as well live it up."

That was what he couldn't understand. Their

one chance? Would there be no others? It was as though everything there was to do, to feel, to see, to hear, to experience had to be crammed into the month of May. Yet what did they do? Mrs. Roberts went off each day to look through church records; Mr. Roberts wandered about with his camera, taking roll after roll of photos for his albums; and Dan was left free to go about the town on his own, exploring. It was crazy.

When they stepped outside the restaurant, a cold drizzle hit their faces.

"I can't believe this!" said Mrs. Roberts. "I just can't believe this! That beautiful sky!"

They made a run for it, Mother between them, and a minute later the drizzle became a steady rain. They went laughing and clattering down the cobble-stone sidewalk, shrieking when they hit a puddle, and arrived wet and wrinkled at their hotel beyond the wall.

"Oh, you've done it now, 'aven't you?" cried Mrs. Harrison when she saw them. "Gone and left your umbrellas, did you? I'll send tea up directly. And towels, too."

As they went up the stairs to their rooms on the second floor, Dan, in the lead, heard his father say, "You're going tomorrow, then? Do they know you're coming?"

"Yes, I called."

Dan waited for them on the landing. "Who, Mom?"

"Oh, some distant relatives of Brian's. We heard about them through his cousin. They live south of here in Selby—two elderly women. I thought I'd go down and talk with them. They might be able to tell me a lot about the history of the Robertses."

"Why can't we all go?"

"It would be boring for you. You and Dad can keep each other company while I'm gone. And tomorrow night we'll take a boat ride on the river if it doesn't rain again."

Dan went into his own room and changed out of his wet clothes. It was a narrow room with only one window—a former broom closet, he imagined—and there was nothing particularly inviting about it, so he usually went downstairs in the evenings to wait while his parents finished in the bath.

There was a hall around the corner from the reception desk with a frayed carpet on the floor, a grandfather clock in one corner, and several armchairs placed at various angles where women waited for cabs or men sat and smoked of an evening.

Dan enjoyed the smell of it—the smell of old carpeting, of musty upholstery, of wet umbrellas and furniture polish and the fragrance of tea that drifted in occasionally from the dining room across the way. He liked the murmur of voices at the reception desk, the polite exchange of pleasantries from guests going in or out, the chatter of the porters. . . .

He let the big chair envelop him. The springs had worn out and seemed to sink almost to the floor when he sat down, but he didn't mind. He opened his notebook and, with the help of a travel guide, began a new paragraph in his essay on the history of York:

Eboracum, the Roman fortification, was built from the same basic design upon which all Roman forts were built. Within the walls, the site was crossed by two streets, the via praetoria *and the* via principalis. *Today the streets of Petergate and Stonegate lie over these Roman roads, and York Minster, the Cathedral, stands over the Roman Praetorium, or headquarters.*

The tall clock in one corner chimed nine times. Dan remembered the wall in the cellar of the Treasurer's House through which the ghosts of the soldiers had supposedly marched, and then he remembered the window, the dankness, and the fear. Perhaps, as a journalist, he should be recording this, too. He flipped to the back of his notebook and scribbled:

I've felt it every morning now about the time I reach the river. I think it's the Tower, though. It seems to be the Tower. The feeling is more like dread than fear, though I'm not sure of the difference. A foreboding, maybe. An overwhelming certainty that something's going to happen and that my folks know it. It doesn't make sense. And then, this morning, at the cellar window in the Treasurer's House, it was the strongest it's ever been. The fear is a physical thing; it almost makes me sick. And then it's gone as suddenly as it comes.

A shadow fell across his paper, and Dan looked up. Mr. Stanton had come in the front door and walked over to the reception desk, momentarily blocking the light from a dusty lamp on the wall behind him. Leaning over the desk, he was barely visible from where Dan sat.

"I'll not be available tomorrow, Mrs. Harrison," Dan heard him say. "I'll be driving Mrs. Roberts to Selby and don't know how long she'll fancy staying."

"Going to see *them,* is she?"

"That she is, mum."

"Well, then, I hope it's worth 'er cab fare. Some folks would pay for the privilege of *not* going, if you want the truth."

Mr. Stanton turned toward the door again, his profile silhouetted against the light. He paused a moment to pull up the collar of his raincoat. As one of the porters entered the front door, a gust of wind whipped Mr. Stanton's coat about his legs, and shadows danced on the floor between him and the chair where Dan sat. With gray cap, gray hair, and long gray coat, he seemed an apparition indeed. The cold air from outside and the steam from the dining room collided there in the hallway, making a mist that seemed to dissolve skin, cloth, and leather into one ghostly creation.

A sudden rush of rain pelted the windows, and lowering his head and holding onto the bill of his cap, Mr. Stanton moved quickly out the door again and disappeared into the night.

2

THERE WAS a place where the cabbies gathered a few blocks from the hotel. Dan discovered it two days later on his way back from Monk Bar. He had stood on the wall a long time beside the arched gateway, staring up at the hideous figures on top, each holding a rock as though ready to hurl his missile down upon anyone daring to enter from the east road.

There were times, when Dan stared long enough without blinking, that the carved heads seemed to move slightly, the eyes rolling about in their sockets, fixing at last upon him. He would continue to stare until his own eyes became blurred, at which point the figures turned once more to stone. It was an illusion he rather enjoyed.

On his way back to the hotel, he cut through an alley and came upon a small lot behind a pub where benches were strung out under the eaves. Two drivers were washing their cabs at a pump. One was Joe Stanton, whom Dan hardly recognized because his gray hair had fallen down over his forehead.

"Well, then!" Mr. Stanton straightened up and smiled at him, squeezing out his rag on the flagstones. "How's the roving reporter?"

Dan shrugged, hands in his pockets. "Looking for something to do," he said. He wanted to ask Mr. Stanton about Selby, but thought better of it. So he said, "Need any help?"

"The scrubbing's all done, but she could use polishing a bit."

As Dan took the cloth, he had the feeling that it had all happened before—that at some time in the past he had stood face to face with the man in front of him. It was as though reality was simply a repetition of a dream once dreamed. Yet he couldn't remember it as a dream. It was only when something happened that it seemed familiar.

He began with the windshield, leaning over the hood and gently lifting the wipers to dry underneath. There wasn't a dent in the cab anywhere. Every so often, Mr. Stanton would step back to look it over, and then attack a remaining smudge, pressing down hard on the cloth with both hands. Once their eyes met, and Dan felt sure that Joe was about to say something. But then the deep blue eyes looked down again, and the moment was lost.

A red-faced driver sitting near the back door of the pub watched with amusement. "Ought to 'ave a big umbrella, Joe, to put over 'er when it rains." He chuckled. "You'd think the Queen 'erself was goin' to go riding up to the Minster in Stanton's cab."

A second driver at the pump smiled, too. "If the rain don't get it, Joe, the gypsies will. Sam saw them on the north road yesterday. Ambrose Faw will be on the town tonight, you can guess."

Sam, the red-faced driver, laughed and lifted his mug of ale to his lips, then set it back on his knee. "They was down below Aldborough, so it won't take 'em long to get 'ere. Once the Faws is in town, they'll be following the milkman, gettin' the cream fast as 'e's puttin' it out. Won't be a shop in York that 'as milk on the stoop tomorrow if the gypsies come."

Mr. Stanton smiled, but his face was thoughtful, and Dan watched him across the hood of the cab.

"Ambrose ever take the milk off your doorstep, Sam?" he asked, without turning around.

"Not mine, but I've 'eard tales . . ."

"How about you, Dudley?" Mr. Stanton said to the other driver. "The Faws ever take the wheels off your cab? The wipers, even?"

"No, can't say they have. But you know the stories . . ."

"So I've only the rain to look out for, then."

A quiet fell over the lot then. Sam went on drinking, and Dudley went back to work. There was no sound but the sparrows in the eaves and the squeak of Dan's cloth on the hubcaps. There was something commanding about Joe Stanton. He was soft-spoken where the others were rowdy, slight where the others were stout, and yet he gave the feeling of enormous strength. He looked a little like Dan's history teacher back in Pennsylvania. Maybe this was what gave Dan the impression that he had seen the man before. Probably nothing more to it than that. And yet, the strange way that Joe Stanton looked at him sometimes, as though he too were trying to remember. . . .

"How about a glass of shandy, Dan?" Joe was saying, buttoning his shirt cuffs and slipping on his tweed jacket. "Mum wouldn't mind that, would she?"

Always Mum. Nobody ever seemed to refer to his father, because it was Mother who made all the arrangements, Mother who had gone to Selby; Mother who seemed driven by something that Dan could not understand.

"Dad wouldn't," Dan replied and sat down on the bench beside Sam while Mr. Stanton went inside.

Taking advantage of his absence, Dudley came over and picked up his glass from the window ledge.

"Soft on the tinkers, that's what he is," he said and took a drink.

"Arrest the Roms and burn their *vardos*, that's what I say," said Sam. "That'll put an end to the poaching and duckering. Ambrose Faw—why there's 'ardly a man in York don't know the name. The Faws, the Coopers, the Boswells, the Drapers . . . A'ave done with the lot, and England won't miss 'em."

Dudley looked down at Dan. "Friend of Joe's? American, from the sound of you."

"From Pennsylvania. Mr. Stanton drove us to the hotel when we first got here."

Dudley leaned against a post, turning his glass around in his large hands. "Well, he's okay, Joe is. He's a different sort, but a decent bloke."

"That 'e is," agreed Sam. " 'E's a York man, through and through. Most of us, we've come from some other place, you know. My people come up from Bedford, and Dudley's come from Derby. But Joe—far back as 'e knows, 'is was York people—the Danes, maybe. Who knows?"

Joe Stanton came out then on the back step with two glasses in his hands and gave one to Dan. Dan looked up at the face with the deepset eyes and high cheekbones. Despite its frailty, the jaw was square, the neck straight, the eyes proud, and Dan decided that Joe's ancestors could well have stood at the helm of a Viking ship or marched, with plumed helmets, through the gates of Eboracum.

MR. AND MRS. ROBERTS went out for a walk alone that evening, so Dan bathed first. The large tub ("Big enough for the Harvard Rowing Club," said his father) perched on a platform so that one almost had to climb, rather than step, into it. The water gurgled when the faucet was turned and came out hesitantly in fits and starts. But the water in the English toilet varoomed when the chain was pulled, racing around and around the bowl in a whirlpool before it disappeared down the pipe with a monstrous sucking sound. The first time Dan's father had pulled the chain, they had watched the performance in awe; and then Mr. Roberts had said, "Let that be a lesson, Dan: never stick your foot in there," and they'd laughed.

Dan thought about his father as he settled down in the tub. His bony knees stuck up above the surface like islands, and he let the soap float back and forth between them.

He hadn't realized how funny his father could be —not the belly-laugh kind of humor—but remarks that made you chuckle when he said them and smile when you thought about them again later.

He spread his hands out, one on each knee, and surveyed the knobby knuckles, the long fingers, the oval nails. His father's hands, too. And later, when he stood in front of the mirror to dry, he squinted till his eyes were mere slits, observing the face before him. Yes, he could almost see his father's features—the high forehead, the brown eyes, the full lips . . . He didn't look much at all like his mother, in fact, with her green eyes and stubby nose.

He heard his parents enter the adjoining bedroom.

"Dan, you in there?" his father called.

"Yeah. Be out in a minute."

"No hurry."

He finished drying, put on his robe, and flushed the toilet just for the fun of it. Then he turned out the light and padded across the hall to his own small room.

The moonlight streamed in through the small

squares of glass that formed the upper pane of his window, and the same rectangles fell on his bed. He put one foot up on the spread. The squares fell on his foot. Impulsively he lay down full length and lifted his head to see the same pattern on his body. Weird.

He remembered suddenly that he hadn't brushed his teeth and went back to the bathroom without turning on the light. He had just put his hand on the faucet when he heard his father saying,

"There's no point in telling him now, Ruth. There's not a thing he can do about it."

"Brian, he's got to know!"

"Why? He's not getting married tomorrow, is he? Let him enjoy this trip, for God's sake."

Dan stood at the sink, his hand frozen on the knob.

"But he knows there's something wrong. He's not stupid. What he said the other day—about everybody being so secretive. The longer we keep it from him, the more it builds up in his mind. No telling what he imagines—something really awful, I suppose."

There was silence for a moment, and then Dan heard his father say dully, "*Is* there anything worse, Ruth?"

"Oh, Brian!" There was a soft movement in the next room, and Dan could tell, from the way his mother's voice was muffled, that her lips were against his father's face. "There's an equal chance that it *won't* happen, you know. We keep forgetting that."

"That's why I don't want to tell him. It would get

him all upset and maybe, in the end, for nothing. I'm living on that fifty percent hope, Ruth."

His mother was crying now. "I try, Brian. But I'm so scared sometimes."

"I know. . . ."

There were footsteps in the bedroom, and not knowing where they were headed, Dan fled silently back to his own room and softly closed the door. His heart ticked rapidly against the wall of his chest, like a time bomb.

A strange sense of excitement came over him, and he considered the possibility that his father was in trouble of some sort. Bankruptcy, perhaps? Embezzlement? Was that why the trip had been planned so hastily? Was it possible, in fact, that it was even more serious—that his father wasn't an insurance actuary at all, and that this trip involved espionage?

He leaned heavily against the door, his mind racing on ahead of him. His parents were *both* agents. Why else would his mother be willing to spend her vacation looking up records? What was his father really photographing when he went out each morning with his camera? And Mr. Stanton—was he in on it, too? What was the real reason he had taken Dan's mother to Selby yesterday, and what had Mrs. Harrison meant when she'd said, "Going to see *them*, is she?"

But it didn't fit together all that easily. It didn't entirely explain the silences, or the look in his father's eyes.

Brian, he's got to know . . . he's not getting married tomorrow. . . . Is there anything worse? . . . Oh, Brian, I'm so scared. . . .

The momentary excitement gave way to the more familiar foreboding, and Dan went over to the window in the darkness and looked down on the street. They weren't going to tell him until they were ready, that was certain, so to heck with it all. If they wanted to keep it to themselves, let them.

But worry could not be dismissed so lightly. It refused to go away.

On the sidewalk below, a figure stood off in the shadows. Dan opened the window wider and leaned out. It was only a porter having a smoke. From his window he could see over the wall and into the heart of York—could see the lights going out all over the city, and Micklegate Bar, dark and forbidding, silhouetted against the night sky. Somewhere, according to Sam the cabbie, the gypsies were approaching York from the north, and Ambrose Faw would be upon the town.

Sam was wrong. When Dan went out the next morning, the usual bottles of cream stood on the steps of each shop. If Ambrose had come in the night, he had obviously missed these.

Mr. Stanton delivered more guests to the hotel when the nine forty-seven pulled in from Aberdeen. Dan was waiting for him on the steps, though he wasn't sure why.

"Busy today, Dan?" Joe called as he put some bags on the sidewalk. "Thought you might want to take a bit of a ride."

Dan stood up and went over. "Where you going?"

"The missus has some pots need mending, and I'm out to look for the Faws."

Dan looked at him curiously. "You know them?"

"Yes, for a long time."

"Sure, I'd like to go."

"Think you should tell your mum first?"

"She's gone for the day. Dad, too. I'm on my own till dinner."

"Well, then."

Joe swung the cab around in the street, the pots and pans clanking about in the back, and headed north, through the heart of the city and out the other side at Bootham Bar.

"How do you know where to find them?" Dan asked.

"The gypsies are like a calendar. You can tell the day of the month, almost, by where they're camping —Faws, especially. They've been following the same circuit year in, year out, since I've first known them, and that was many years ago."

There was obviously a story to it, and Dan waited, but Mr. Stanton said no more.

"Sam and Dudley don't seem to like them very much. . . ." Dan ventured finally.

Joe grunted. "Sam and Dudley don't know a Romany from a tinker. Ambrose doesn't even come into town anymore. Used to be we'd hear his knock on the gate, the wife and I, and we'd gather up the knives to be sharpened or the chairs to be mended. He could do almost anything. Now we have to seek the gypsies out."

Why?"

"They've got a name put on them, that's why. I'm not saying Ambrose never took a chicken that didn't belong to him, or that he never traded off a lame horse. He's done all that and more, I suppose, but nothing like they say he does. When word gets out that the gypsies are around, the thieves get busy, knowing that the blame'll fall to the Faws. It's been said that if you want to knife a man, you wait till the gypsies reach the north road and you'll go free. Ambrose knows that, so he keeps to himself."

The magic sound of words: Ambrose Faw. The syllables had a sinister ring about them, as though invoking the name would bring the dreaded gypsy himself. Fagan, from *Oliver Twist,* rose up in Dan's imagination, and he could feel his pulse beating where his wrists rested against his thighs.

"There are gypsies and then there are gypsies, of course," Mr. Stanton continued. "Some of them—Hedgecrawlers, that's what Ambrose calls them—they're too idle to stir themselves. All they want is to lie about; a drink and a smoke will do. There are some that leave their litter after they move on, and some that will take a body's wash off the line. But a

33

man doesn't have to be gypsy to take what isn't his The Faws, though, are true Romanies—true travelers. If it weren't for the ashes of their fire, you wouldn't know the Faws had passed that way."

"You're never afraid of them, then?"

"Afraid?" Joe gave him a sudden, sharp look "What's there to see in a gypsy's face you don't see in your own? They've put their horses in a farmer's field overnight to graze, that's sure, and they may have picked his apples too on the sly. But they don't snatch babies out of carriages and go off with them, like some people would have you believe, or test their knives on a man's throat. You listen to Sam and Dudley and you'd think the Faws came in through Bootham Bar at midnight looking for heads, that's what you'd think." He grunted again and grew still.

The road dipped and turned as it headed toward the Yorkshire Wolds. Small villages were scattered here and there as though they'd been planted by the wind. The cab would go over the brink of a desolate hill to descend sharply between cottages and an inn. Then, just as suddenly, the houses gave way to the moors again, and heather and bracken stretched as far as the eye could see.

"I wish I'd brought my notebook," Dan said suddenly.

"They wouldn't take to that—someone writing about them, you know."

"I guess not." Dan was silent for a time, but at last the reporter in him got the upper hand. "How did you first come to know them?"

34

Joe Stanton smiled slightly. "I've known the name Faw all my life, because there've always been Faw gypsies in the north country. But the truth is, I knew Ambrose when I was a lad. He'd come to town with his father and clean our chimney or set to work on anything we had for them to do. I'd hang around and talk to Ambrose, and it got so that when they came back our way every six weeks or so, my mum would let me camp with them a day or two before they moved on. I learned some of the Romany words, ate the gypsy stew, slept out under the stars. . . ."

"And you've stayed friends all these years?"

Mr. Stanton's smile dimmed a little. "Well, we see each other. There was a while I wasn't so welcome in the *vardo,* the wagon. I fell for his sister. Polly, that was her name. It was hard to tell how she felt about me. She liked me, I think—always smiling. Teasing, you might say. But her father wasn't happy at all. Didn't want any of his daughters marrying a *gorgio;* and the next time I went to see them, they were gone and didn't come our way again for two years. When they did come, Polly had a husband with her, and a baby too, so that was the end of it. Then Ambrose married a girl named Rose and joined his wife's clan —bought himself an old bow-top *vardo* and fixed it up. Sometimes I'd go help him work on it. Fanciest thing you ever saw, it was. Well, not now. It's old and in need of paint, but you should have seen it then. . . . So we keep in touch."

There was a twinkle in Joe's eyes. "Also, you see, Ambrose and I have the same fortune. His mother-in-law read our fortunes years ago. She said that whatever ill luck befell one of us would befall the other; whatever happiness, the other would experience, too. The day of our deaths, she said, was already written in the stars. So it's best, you see, we keep an eye out for each other."

"Has she been right so far?" Dan asked.

"Well, she has and she hasn't. We're both alive, so maybe it's too early to tell. On the other hand, the wife and I always wanted children, but there were none born to us, whereas Ambrose and Rose had four. Yet I suppose I could count up four happinesses the missus and I have had that Ambrose and Rose haven't. So it all evens out, I guess."

"You've always been a cab driver?"

"Not always, but it seems to suit me. As a lad, I wanted to be a scholar, a history teacher. I was good at the books. I read all sorts of things I didn't have to. I've always had a special feel for York, you see. She stands here knowing more than she can ever tell us, and it's up to us to ferret out her secrets. No game was ever as exciting to me as searching for the ancient parts of the city, as learning to tell which portions of the wall were Roman and which were medieval. Every time a new dig is begun, a new discovery made, it fills me with excitement. For me, the city and its walls and its streets are alive. There is no dead thing here. It used to be that I could put my hand on the wall and feel the vibration of soldiers' marching feet. I could stand in the Tower and hear, dimly, the soldiers' voices calling out a salute to their emperor. It sounds mad, I know. . . ."

"No," Dan said thoughtfully, "it doesn't sound mad at all. Did you become a professor, then?"

"It never came about. My father died early and it was up to me to support my mother and sisters. The university was out of the question. I got jobs here and there and ended up buying a cab and squiring people about. My knowledge of the city, though, has made it a good living, and I'm a tour guide as much as a driver. It was not the living I had in mind, but it fills a need, and the missus and I are comfortable."

Dan hesitated. "And do you ever put your hand on the wall now, or listen for voices in the Tower?"

A mask seemed to fall over Joe's face, for it lost all expression. "I haven't time for that now," he said simply.

They turned off the country road onto an even narrower lane with a stone fence on either side. Joe drove more cautiously, rounding the hedges slowly; and suddenly, straight ahead, Dan saw an old woman pushing a small cart loaded with sticks, her back to them. A small child held onto her skirt. Several dogs were milling about, and half a dozen chickens scrabbled in the dirt. The old woman turned when she heard the car approaching and removed the pipe from her mouth.

"Oy, oy, oy," she cried, waving her apron at the chickens, and they strutted, clucking, off to one side.

Mr. Stanton pulled slowly up beside her and tipped his cap.

"How do, Granny?" he said, and she squinted at him a moment, then smiled broadly, her open mouth toothless and black.

The cab went on up the road toward a red wagon trimmed in gold and green that was parked off on one side. It had a round top and ornate carving at both ends. A set of curved steps, propped between the wagon shafts, led to the curtained door. Horses and ponies were tethered by the roadside, munching the long grass. Brightly colored clothing was strewn about on the hedge, drying in the sun.

A young boy called out, "Joe!" and grinned as the cab came to a stop. The mother and sister smiled shyly from around the *vardo*. Joe opened the door and got out.

Dan reached for the handle on his side and started to follow when suddenly his eyes met those of a huge man standing with arms folded. His blackish-gray hair was long and flowing, and he wore a purple band around his forehead. His eyes were black, fierce under the bushy brows. His long nose flared at the bottom where it curled down, hiding the nostrils, and there was a slight kink in the middle. A black mustache all but covered his mouth, matching his brows; but beneath the mouth, a gray beard, wild and frizzled, extended down onto his chest. He wore a checkered shirt and an old suit coat that did not match his trousers. Several chains, gold or brass, hung around

his neck. There were small wrinkles about the eyes—
wrinkles that might have been laugh lines. But the
man was not laughing, and Dan knew that he was
looking into the face of Ambrose Faw.

It was not until Mr. Stanton came around the cab
that the gypsy moved. The two men clasped each
other's hand, held it a minute, then let go. The laugh
lines about Ambrose Faw's eyes deepened, and finally
he was smiling. He led Joe to the *vardo* and poured
him a glass of something dark.

"To the road," said Joe, holding up his glass.

"Your health," said Ambrose, and they drank.

The ceremony over, the rest of the family came
forward. By now the old grandmother had reached
the camp with her cart of firewood, and the small
child scampered over to Ambrose and clung to his
leg.

Dan, watching from the cab, counted seven people in all, including a young man who hung back in
the shadows. Ambrose's children seemed to vary
widely in age.

"I've brought a boy along," Joe was saying. "Dan,
bring the pots over, eh?"

Dan was glad he had been introduced that way,
relieved that he had something to do. And yet, as he
took the pots from the cab and laid them on the grass,
he could feel the gypsies' eyes on him—studying,
measuring, calculating. . . .

Ambrose bent down to examine the handles, and

Joe pointed out a large kettle that had burned through on the bottom.

"That one, too?" he asked. "You can fix it?"

"Yes. In a few days."

"Good." Joe turned then and put one hand on Dan's shoulder. "This is Dan Roberts, from the States. Helping me out today."

Ambrose's wife, Rose, held the bottle out toward Dan and smiled. "*Piv?*" she offered.

"I think perhaps not," said Joe, answering for him, and then introduced the others to Dan: Jasper, the young man in the shadows; Orlenda, a girl of sixteen, maybe; Nat, the boy, a few years younger; and Rachel, the smallest. The old granny busied herself behind the *vardo*. She wanted no part of introductions.

"Nat," Joe said, turning again to the boy. "How many dogs do you have now?"

The boy smiled broadly. "Five," he said, and made a sound with his lips that brought all the dogs to him where they stood quietly.

Dan knelt down and put out his hand. One of the dogs came over and licked it. This seemed to please the Faws.

"You've a *juckel?*" Nat asked him.

Dan tried to understand.

"A dog," Joe interpreted.

"No, I don't."

"You should have a *juckel,*" said Nat. And then the gypsies fell silent again.

Dan stood up self-consciously. He was used to rolling conversations, where one sentence followed on the period of another. The Faws were all watching him; their features seemed to mingle into one dark face with a dozen eyes—eyes like ripe olives—all looking at him, all watching. Orlenda was leaning against the *vardo,* bare feet crossed at the ankles. She was laughing, amused, but made no sound when she laughed. Why did he feel that he had been here before? Dan wondered. Why did he feel as though he were seeing them again, when he had never, he knew, even dreamed them? What was it Ambrose was thinking when he fastened his dark eyes on Dan's? And all the while Jasper watched from the edge of the trees.

The grandmother squatted by the fire.

"Stay and have a bite with us," Ambrose said, as the old woman stirred the contents of the kettle with a stick. Joe answered by sitting down and lighting his pipe, and so it was agreed.

Dan did not want to stay, but he had no choice. He went over to where the young man was standing and sat down, but Jasper immediately moved away. Nat took his brother's place.

"Jasper's a mute," he explained, nodding in the direction of his older brother.

"Oh, I didn't know."

"How could you? He didn't tell you, did he?" the boy said simply, and laughed.

"He's always been that way?" Dan asked, struggling to keep the conversation going, since Joe and Ambrose were engaged in talk of their own.

"Since a wee *chavvy*, I guess, before I was born. Mum says he was *trashed* once, and that did it."

"Trashed?"

"Scared. Maybe a *gavver* caught him, hit him in the head. Who knows? Hasn't been right since, you know."

Dan fell silent, hopelessly muddled.

Nat reached out and ran one finger over on the buckle of Dan's belt. It was a fancy buckle made of copper, ornately decorated with the head of an eagle, its sharp beak forming the prong.

"I'll trade for this," he said.

Dan smiled. "I can't. It's the only belt I brought with me. I wouldn't have anything to hold my pants up."

Orlenda found it all very amusing. She seemed to find everything amusing, Dan decided. She ducked her head, then lifted it again and went on watching, standing in the same position, her slim ankles crossed, her feet deeply tanned. She was holding some dry reeds, which she was weaving into a basket. Every so often she would reach behind her on the narrow porch of the *vardo* and take another willow, which her nimble fingers deftly blended into the rest.

The old grandmother got up and went over to Joe, holding out her pipe, and he filled it with tobacco. She grinned at him again with her darkened mouth and then went off by herself to smoke. The mute had sat down on the opposite bank across the road and was watching the others. Only Rose was left to tend the stew, which simmered now over the hot fire and gave off a pungent aroma.

It was served at last in tin plates that grew hot to the touch and had to be set on the grass. The spices were new to Dan's taste, and the meat had been cut into strange shapes. It was nothing he recognized. He sat looking at it there in his plate and noticed suddenly that Ambrose was watching, his eyes smiling beneath the heavy black brows.

"*Chuchi,*" he said.

Dan looked at him and then at the meat.

"Rabbit, Dan," Joe said, amused, and Dan began to eat, embarrassed that they had seen his hesitation. Afterwards he wiped his hands on the grass as the others did, and when he caught Orlenda laughing again, he smiled back. This time she turned her head quickly over her shoulder, seemingly embarrassed.

This is crazy! Dan thought. It was like a dream sequence where nothing made sense and everything made sense: the mute, eating off to himself; Orlenda, laughing at nothing; the grandmother, surrounded by the smoke of her pipe; the dogs, strangely silent; and through it all, Ambrose's eyes—always watching.

"Still *duckering,* Rose?" Joe asked, turning to Mrs. Faw.

"Aye, but the ladies come to me now. I don't go into town and let them talk behind my back. Yesterday a fine lady drove out in a big car. I told her she would soon lose all her money, and she turned as white as ashes."

Joe smiled. "She'll not be coming back if you tell her that."

"Aye, but she will. I said there was only one man who could help her get her wealth back again, but I wouldn't have his name 'til tomorrow."

They all laughed then.

"How do you read the future?" Dan asked, curious.

Rose studied him. "The palm of the hand, the leaves in a cup, the eyes, the stars . . ."

"Read Dan's hand, Mother," Orlenda said, and because it was the first time she had spoken, Dan looked at her, wondering.

Mrs. Faw smiled and reached for Dan's hand. "He will take a long trip," she joked, without even looking at it. "He will go to America some day."

They all found that amusing, and Dan laughed with them. Then, more seriously, Mrs. Faw placed Dan's hand over hers, palm up, and examined it carefully. Dan, watching her face, saw her warm smile give way slowly until there was no smile at all on her lips.

"No," she said suddenly, dropping his hand, "one cannot give a proper fortune to a boy under twenty. Come back, Dan, when you are thirty-five—forty, even—and I will tell it to you then."

She leaned forward and poked at the fire, but long after the others had begun talking again, she sat very still, her dark eyes on Dan.

3

THE DULL GREENISH-BROWN of bracken again. The cab made its way back over the country roads to York. Dan was glad to be leaving, and yet it seemed as though something of himself were left behind—that he would not be complete until he went again. For now, however, he welcomed the relief of getting away. Looking about him, he wondered at the muted colors.

Was this the southern border of the fierce Brigantes, bearers of the blue war-shields, and the tribes of the Painted People, whom the Romans had been sent to conquer? Was this the way the land had looked to the legionaries when they marched northward— the soft gray landscape mingling with the mist that rolled in over the moors from the sea?

How could he write all this in his essay so the teacher could see the heather, smell the earth, and feel the dampness of the fog upon the skin? What words could he use, and in what sequence, to bring this road, this place, to life on the written page? The words were there; they were always there, awaiting only the touch of the writer to make them live. Would he be such a writer? And how many years would it take? The future was always on the other side of college—graduate school, even. The nice thing about being old must be that you'd already had your future, your chance. For better or worse, nobody could take it away from you.

He realized suddenly that they were halfway back to York. If he was going to ask Mr. Stanton the question that had been shaping itself since morning, he'd better do it now. It might be his only chance. He had to phrase it carefully, ask it right the first time.

"Joe," he said, "how are those women getting along—the ones Mother went to see in Selby?"

If Joe was startled by the question, he didn't show it. His eyes never left the road. "The Welles sisters, you mean? No better, no worse, I suppose. I didn't go in this time. 'Twas your mother's visit."

At least I know their name, Dan thought, and wondered what to ask next.

"So what did you do all day? Mom was there a long time."

"Oh, a bit of this and that. Went to a pub. I'm a bit like the gypsies, Dan. Wherever I am, I make myself comfortable."

"Didn't Mother want you to go in with her?"

"Why should she? The sick one doesn't bite, you

know. She's got her sister there to care for her. It was nice of your mum to call. Few folks do. They're relatives, then?"

"I guess so. Distant relatives." Dan waited. "You've met them before?"

At first Joe didn't answer, but finally he said, "Once . . . twice a year, maybe . . . I drive down to Selby to see them—take them some eggs or fruit, you know. . . ." His voice trailed off.

But Dan sensed a story and wouldn't let it be.

"Are you friends with them, then?"

"I only know them through my father, and the story's not a pleasant one." Joe glanced over at him, hesitated, and then looked out over the road again. "I never saw them till I was a young man, and then 'twas only their house. My father pointed it out to me. He was ashamed of the story, but he wanted me to know it. Years before, you see, the Welles family lived in York, and there was something wrong in that family. Nobody knew just what. The local folk, they call it the 'magrums'—a sickness, I guess it is. But they didn't understand it, nor do I. There's a proper name for it, I'm sure. The old father had it first. Folks used to say it was caused by the witches, like maybe the old woman had put a hex on her husband. And then when one of the daughters came down with it, people started acting as though maybe she was the witch— taunting her when she went outside—throwing sticks at her, tripping her, even. And my father, I'm afraid, was one of them. Old Mrs. Welles decided she'd had

47

enough and moved her family to Selby where she and Elizabeth, the healthy daughter, nursed the others. The old folks died eventually, which just left Lizzie and Pearl to fend for themselves. They never go outside, the daughters. When Lizzie has need of something, she has it delivered. All the folks in Selby know of Pearl is that she's poorly.

"When my father was grown, what he did as a boy began to weigh heavily on him, and he began driving down to Selby every so often with a basket of groceries for the family. But he never went inside, just set it by the door. Ashamed to show his face, he was, to Lizzie, after the way he'd teased her sister. So now I go, but I go inside, take a cup of tea with them, chat a little with Lizzie, and go off again. Lizzie, she knows who I am, but she never mentions my father, and I never mention the sickness. She thanks me for the butter and the eggs and the fruit and I tell her I'll be back that way again. And that's the way it's been all these years. My missus, she says it's the least I can do. . . ."

It was too plausible not to believe—a story of guilt and goodness, of remorse and retribution. Dan felt strangely comforted. Obviously his mother had wanted to spare him the unpleasantness of meeting the Welles sisters, their long-distant relatives, knowing, perhaps, that one of them was ill. She didn't want anything to spoil this trip. There was probably nothing more to it than that. Her whispered comment to Dan's father on the stairs, Mrs. Harrison's remark at the desk, it all made sense now. . . . And yet? But Dan was relieved, and he felt better about Joe, too. A gentleness showed on the man's face as he leaned his arms on the steering wheel, and Dan wanted to see more of him before they left York.

"I'm glad you asked me to come today," he said. "Could I go back with you when you pick up the pots?"

"Sure, glad to have the company."

As Dan walked up the steps to the hotel, he realized that he had avoided asking Joe anything more about Ambrose. It seemed terribly strange, now that he thought about it, and he wondered if he was afraid.

Mrs. Harrison was at the desk when he came in, and raised one eyebrow. "Out 'aving a bit of a ride with Joe, eh?" she said. "Well, you'd better tell your father next time where you're off to. He saw you ride away this morning and asked me about it. Wasn't a thing I could tell him now, was there?"

Dan went on upstairs. His parents' room was empty. Their jackets were gone—also his father's camera and his mother's notebook, so he knew they were still out. It was only two fifteen, and they would not be going to dinner till late.

Suddenly, the relief he had felt earlier evaporated and the worries returned. There were still too many unanswered questions. He remembered the strange conversation he had overheard in his parents' room, and all at once he felt that he had to know.

Even as he thought about it and what he was about to do, his pulse quickened. Whatever the secret was, whatever awful thing they had kept hidden, shouldn't he be in on it? If it affected their lives, didn't it affect his also? Didn't he have a right to find out?

He had never searched his parents' things before. There had never been a reason. There had always been trust. Trust and respect. And he found that now—slipping his fingers into the inner pockets of his father's sport jackets—there was a strange crawling sensation in his throat, a rapid beating of his heart. Was it because of what he was doing or because of what he might find? His fingers closed around his father's passport and he took it out, examining it carefully. The name, the birthdate—all the information seemed to be in order. No secret agent here. If his father were living under an assumed name, he'd been doing so all his life. Dan continued searching, pulling out restaurant receipts, a candy wrapper, a railway timetable. . . .

He felt more anxious, somehow, going through his mother's dresser drawers. Most of her things were in her purse, he reasoned, but still there must be something left behind, something to give him a clue.

He turned to look at her briefcase there by the bed and sat down, perspiration on his palms. If he was caught going through their clothes in the closet, he could always say he was looking for gum or Kleenex or change. But what possible excuse was there for going through a briefcase?

His head throbbed with a fearful expectancy. He had to know. Slowly he put his hand inside and pulled out a number of envelopes. All letters, it seemed, bound together with a rubber band. All were from relatives, but most of them from Dad's cousin, Donna Roberts. Again he put his hand in the briefcase and came out with a stack of documents, copies of immigration papers, birth certificates. It was just as Mother had said, family records. He had seen some of the papers at home, and all seemed reasonable and proper. There was even a sketchy drawing of the Roberts' family tree. Daniel unfolded the paper and spread it out on the bed.

He had seen the sketch before. His mother had shown it to him, in fact. But this time something about it was different. A number of names had been circled. And beneath his father's name, and Donna's, and Kitty's, and his Aunt Shirley's, a question mark.

Dan stared at it in confusion. What did it mean? What was the significance of the circles and the question marks? Perhaps Brian Roberts wasn't his real father after all. Perhaps Dan was adopted, but how could that be? He looked like his father: the same long face, the same lean body, the forehead, the eyes. . . .

There was a click of a door behind him, and Dan whirled around. Brian Roberts entered the room. Neither of them spoke. Neither moved. They each seemed frozen until Mr. Roberts' eyes scanned the family tree on the bed. Slowly he took the camera

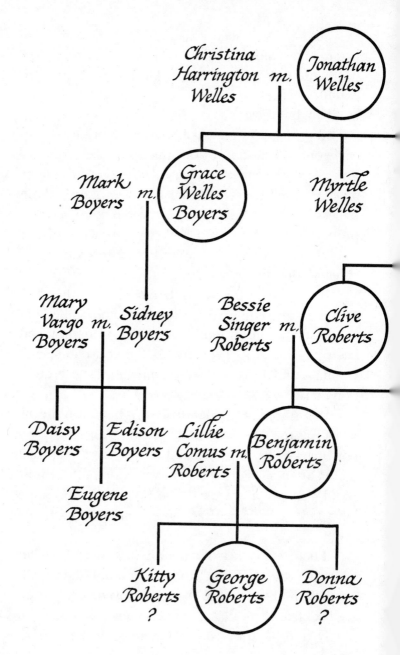

Dan's Family Tree

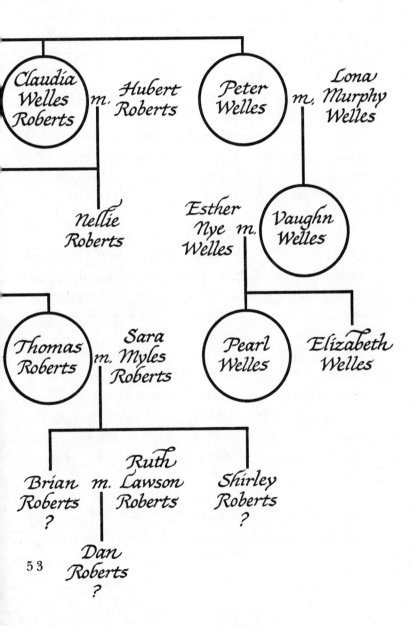

Claudia Welles Roberts m. Hubert Roberts

Peter Welles m. Lona Murphy Welles

Nellie Roberts

Esther Nye Welles m. Vaughn Welles

Thomas Roberts m. Sara Myles Roberts

Pearl Welles

Elizabeth Welles

Brian Roberts ? m. Ruth Lawson Roberts

Shirley Roberts ?

Dan Roberts ?

53

from around his neck, laid it on the dresser, and came over.

"THAT'S YOUR MOTHER'S STUFF, Dan."

"Yeah, I know. But it's my family tree. I didn't think she'd mind."

"What were you looking for?"

"Nothing in particular."

"Well, then, you'd better put it back."

There was a tension in his father's voice that told Dan he was holding something forbidden, something sinister, something that belonged in the briefcase and was never supposed to be let out.

"I'll be careful with it," he answered. "I just want to look it over."

Mr. Roberts didn't answer. He moved to the window, his back to Dan, hands in his pockets. He looked very strange, somehow, like a tire that was slowly deflating—smaller than he had ever seemed before. With each breath that he took, his shoulders sagged a bit lower.

Dan looked at the paper again. Dan Roberts, son of Brian Roberts, son of Thomas Roberts, son of Clive Roberts, son of Hubert Roberts, son of. . . . There was no father given for Hubert. Instead, the family line had switched suddenly to his wife's side. Claudia Welles Roberts, daughter of Jonathan Welles.

"I thought Mom was working on the history of the Roberts' family," Dan said, curious. "How come she switched over to the Welleses?"

There was a long pause, and in that pause, he remembered the Welles sisters in Selby. There they were on the chart, great-granddaughters of Jonathan Welles.

"Maybe she couldn't trace the Robertses back any further. Maybe that's as far as she was able to go."

The answer left too many questions. No, Dan thought, it wasn't the Robertses who interested his mother at all. It was the Welleses. Jonathan's name was the first one circled. Why?

He looked up at his father again. It was as though his dad were anticipating the question, as though the muscles were tensed, awaiting the onslaught, as though every word that was uttered punctured the air and fractured the bones as well.

After all these months, he had found the something he was not supposed to see. He knew the question he was not supposed to ask. His heart raced as he heard himself ask it:

"What do the circles mean, Dad?"

The question was out, and even before the last syllable was uttered, his father had turned to meet it, as though defending himself from a surprise attack.

"Have you ever heard of Huntington's disease, Dan?"

A sickness, then. He had been right. The months of worry, of silence, of unspoken questions. . . . The 'magrums'? Was someone dying, then? He shook his head.

Mr. Roberts sat down in a chair by the window,

leaning forward, arms resting on his knees. The afternoon sun illuminated all the wrinkles, the crow's feet about the eyes, the deeper furrows on each side of the mouth. . . .

"It's a hereditary disease that can be passed along from one generation to the next—that's what the circled names mean; those are the relatives who had it, or whom we suppose had it, from what we could find out in letters, death certificates, stories. . . ." He paused.

Dan looked down at the paper again. "Beginning with Jonathan Welles?" The very name seemed evil.

"Oh, much further back than that. That's as far as Mother's been able to trace it."

Dan was quiet for a moment. Then, "What's it like, the disease?"

"It's a defect in one of the genes that causes destruction of nerve cells in the brain. It produces different symptoms in different people. It was named after the doctor who discovered it . . . who identified it."

"When did you and Mom find out about it?"

"I got a letter last January from my cousin in Wyoming. She told me that her father—my father's brother—had probably not been mentally ill as we had all thought. Last year Donna's brother began showing some of the same symptoms that his father had had, and a doctor told them he suspected Huntington's disease. He asked Donna to check with all her relatives and find out as much as she could about whether others might have had it, too. We've had many phone calls since then . . many letters. . . ."

'Did your father have it?"

'I think so. The last ten years of his life were very difficult for my mother, as we have probably told you. She suspected that he'd been drinking. I was away at college, so I didn't really know. It didn't seem like Dad to take to the bottle, but I took Mother's word for it. I'm sorry now that I did. It must have been frightening and confusing to him as well."

Dan looked down at the chart again. "What about Aunt Shirley?"

"She's fine as far as we know. I haven't wanted to tell her yet—but I'll have to. She has to know."

And the question mark by his father's name?

"You're not sick, are you?" Dan asked, and was conscious of how dry his lips had become.

"I don't think so. I don't feel sick."

"Well, then." Relief surged through Dan. "I don't see why Mom's making such a big deal of it."

Mr. Roberts smiled a little. "She wants to exonerate the family name, that's what. With rumors of alcoholism and mental illness in my family, she said she wanted to find out the truth—so you'd have a dad you were proud of."

"It doesn't make any difference to me what the rest of your family was anyway," said Dan. "It's you that counts."

His father reached over and put his hand on Dan's arm, held it there for a minute, then dropped

5 7

it. "I remember Dad telling me once that *his* father was sick for the last few years of his life, and nobody knew what was wrong with him. I come from a long line of hard-working farmers, see, and country people tend to keep their problems to themselves. But ignorance is a dangerous thing. It's better if you know."

"Then why didn't you tell me about it before? I could take it."

"I should have, I guess. I just didn't want to worry you about it yet."

"What's to worry? I can't get it if you don't have it. Right?"

"Right. If I don't have it. . . ."

Cold fear seized Dan, as though he had missed something before . . . as though the question mark that had been floating about the room had settled suddenly over his own head. "You mean you can still get it?"

"I either have it or I don't, Dan. But it doesn't usually show up until a person is thirty-five or forty. Sometimes even later—fifty. Sixty, even. That's the scary part."

"Well, you're thirty-nine, Dad, and you don't have any symptoms yet. Maybe you won't get any till you're eighty, who knows?"

"I hope that doesn't happen," his father said quietly. "If I'm carrying the gene that causes it, I want to know, so *you* can know." He put his hands over his face. "If I have it, Dan, you'd have a fifty percent chance of having it, too."

It was as though the room were dividing in half
—half light, half shadow. As though the question
mark were descending now, splitting his head in half.
How long would he have to wait to find out? How
long could he go without knowing?

"I want to go to a hospital and get tested," Dan
said, and noticed the strange anger rising in his voice.
"I don't want to go my whole life wondering if I have
it or not. That's crazy. I've got things to do. I've got
college. I want to find out and get it over with."

"I wish you could, Dan. I feel the same way."

The question mark had reached his chest and
was tearing his lungs apart, one from the other.

"Why can't we?"

"Because they don't have an accurate test yet.
There isn't any way we can know. We have to wait it
out."

Why was this worse than knowing he had it? Dan
wondered. Why was the dread deeper, knowing that
maybe—when he was thirty-five or forty . . . ? Because
he couldn't plan? Because there was no future he
could count on?

How did you go about arranging your life with
something hanging over you all the time? How did
you make yourself cram through four years of college
—six, even—knowing that when you finally finished
and got a job, you might have only ten good years
left? How did you even think about having a wife, a
family, knowing that you might be passing the defect
on to your children before it was discovered in yourself?

And suddenly he remembered the dark eyes of Rose Faw, looking at him over the fire. *Come back when you're thirty-five, Dan—forty, even—and I will tell it to you then.*

HE SAT ON THE BANK near Lendal Bridge, his notebook beside him, and watched the cruise boat taking on passengers across the river. He had written just one paragraph:

> *The river is the only constant thing in York. The Romans sailed up the Ouse in shallow-draft ships. Tostig and Harald of Norway followed, to their eventual destruction. Stone for the building of the great Minster was delivered on these waters, and merchants sent their cargoes of wool down the river to the Humber and finally to the sea. . . .*

He remembered the way his father had looked, sitting there by the window, the deep lines etched in his face. He wished he had not left so abruptly, had not picked up his notebook and gone out raging silently. They were in this together, he and his father, and while he had perhaps twenty years to look forward to, his father rejoiced with each new day that passed in good health. To his father, every day held the terrible possibility of a Roman galley coming into view, of plume-helmeted soldiers swarming up the bank, of the blare of a trumpet and the sound of soldiers' feet advancing behind the glitter of swords and shields.

He put his notebook on his knees and picked up his pen again:

When Vespasian was proclaimed emperor, he decided to subdue the warlike tribes of northern Britain. He ordered Quintus Petillius Cerealis to take command of the Ninth Legion, the Hispana, stationed at Lincoln, and move northward. It was at the junction of the Ouse and the Foss Rivers that a fortress, Eboracum, was built in A.D. *71.*

The Ninth Legion consisted of highly trained infantrymen and skilled engineers. Each legion contained five or six thousand men. There were ten cohorts in a legion, six centuries in a cohort, and each century was commanded by an officer called a centurion.

A Roman legionary was expected to march twenty miles in five hours, heavily loaded, to help dig the ditches of a camp in the evening, and to be ready to fight at any time. . . .

Tough. That's what they had to be, he and his father. They had come this far, and nothing had happened yet. They could lick it . . . maybe. . . .

A sudden wave of resentment swept over him, an unreasonable anger toward his father. For thirty-nine years, Brian Roberts had been free of the fear that Dan felt now. Because he had never known about it, he had lived his life as certain of the future as one can ever be. Perhaps it was better not knowing, better to have it just happen to you, like a meteorite falling from the sky or something. What was the chance of a meteorite falling on you? Almost none? What was the chance that he—Dan Roberts—would get Huntington's disease? Fifty out of a hundred—if his father had it.

He raged that he had found it out, at the same time furious that his parents had kept it from him. Better to just see the Roman galley sailing up the Ouse one day without any forewarning than to anticipate it for ten or twenty years, letting it rob you of sleep, of hope, of joy. . . .

He was writing again, and this time his scrawl looked dark and angry there on the paper:

Discipline and punishment in a Roman camp were severe. Sentries who fell asleep at their posts were stoned to death by their comrades. For the cowardice of a unit in battle, every tenth man might be executed. Flogging was common.

A legion commander always tried to fight a battle on ground of his own choosing. He drew his men up in lines facing a charging enemy. Spears were made of metal heads and soft wooden shafts. If these pierced the enemy's armor or shield when they were thrown, the shaft bent and could not easily be pulled out. While the enemy was still reeling under the onslaught of the javelins, the legionaries charged in with their short stabbing swords. . . .

The flash of a fish glittered on the surface of the water. Dan put his notebook down and crept over to the river's edge, watching—waiting to see it again. The river had taken on a rosy hue in the glow of the afternoon sun, and now that the cruise boat had departed, the Ouse was still again, its calm surface a façade for the currents that flowed beneath.

Dan stared at his reflection in the water—a blur, nothing more. It was as though he were looking down upon himself drowning there in the Ouse. He had not thought much about death before. Dying was ' something you did if you were careless and had an accident, or were old and got sick. Or perhaps it was something you did on purpose if you had Huntington's disease and knew what was coming. . . .

He was not thinking about suicide for himself, but wondered if his father ever thought about it. If you could not plan your life, perhaps you could plan your death, do it up right, a smashing success. Perhaps there was something satisfying in that.

As he looked down at the water, he was startled suddenly to see that his own reflection had disappeared, and he was staring into the face of a Roman soldier.

The eyes were small and determined, the nose long and thin, the jaw square. There was a round brass helmet on the soldier's head, with a peak at the back, and cheekpieces that came down on each side as far as the chin. So clear and detailed was the face, unlike his own reflection, that Dan could even see a scar above the nose, a raised place between the brows.

He wheeled around to see if someone was standing over him, but the bank was deserted. When he looked in the water again, his heart pounding, he saw nothing. The slant of the sun on the river had erased it all.

DAN HEADED SHAKILY down North Street and back toward the hotel, clutching his notebook. It had not been a hallucination. It had not been like looking at the figures above Monk Bar, staring at them so long without blinking that they seemed to roll their eyes at him. That was a hallucination. That was an optical trick, an aberration of the mind, a hypnotic suggestion. He knew the difference. And he knew that the face in the water had been as certain, as real, as the fish he had seen only moments before.

He wondered what his parents' reaction would be if he told them, and whether he ought to tell them at all. It would sound insane, he knew, and they might see it as a symptom. What *were* the symptoms of Huntington's disease? Was it possible to have your first attack at the age of fifteen? Pearl Welles must have had the symptoms when she was quite young. Is this what it was like for his father—every abnormality viewed as a premonition of things to come? Was it constantly comparing your performance one day with what you had done the day before to see if there was any change?

He did not know what frightened him most— what he had seen in the water or what it might mean about his mind. The injustice of it made him furious. Why not polio or typhoid or rheumatic fever or tuberculosis, an equal chance for everybody? Why a rare disease that confined itself to preselected families? How could it be that a flaw could flow from past to present to future without end? Without a cure? A face in the water. It must be madness. What else?

He reached the safety of the hotel lobby and sank breathlessly down in one of the overstuffed chairs. The everyday sights and sounds had a calming effect on him: the clink of china from the dining room, the opening and closing of the front door. . . .

Joe Stanton had been taking tea in the restaurant dining room and, seeing Dan, stopped by his chair on the way out.

"I'll probably drive back to the Faws day after tomorrow, Dan," he said. "I'll pick you up that morning."

Perhaps it was the angle at which he viewed him, perhaps it was the events of the day or his state of mind, but Dan seemed to see Joe more clearly than he had ever seen him before. The intense eyes, the nose—long and thin—the square jaw in an otherwise fragile face; and then, something he had never noticed before, a light scar, a raised place, between the brows.

4

D AN LAY TENSELY on his bed, staring up at the
ceiling, one foot resting on the floor, ready
to spring.

Thoughts spun wildly in his head: dodging each
other, rising, falling, colliding, then whirling once
more out of control.

He tried to test his faculties one by one as a
check for sanity; memory: what he had for breakfast
today, yesterday, and the day before; computations:
the square root of 676 divided by four. If ten
angels could dance on the head of a pin, and one
angel could dance on the point, would you say
that. . . ?

The fear was too great. He had looked into the
River Ouse that afternoon to see the beginnings of
his own demise. Was it possible for a son to get symptoms of the disease before the parent?

The handle of his door turned, and Dan sat up

quickly, only to see his mother enter. He lay back, arms over his forehead.

"Dan?" She did not even come over, just stood in one spot, aware of the tension, afraid of it. "You feeling okay?"

The anxiety in her voice; this is the way it would be from now on. Any show of depression on his part would increase it tenfold for them.

"Yes." His voice was dull.

She moved then, coming over to sit on the edge of the bed. Dan pulled up his leg to make room for her. He was glad, really, that she was there.

"We'll be going to dinner after a while—when you're ready."

"Okay."

But still she stayed.

"Brian told me about this afternoon. I thought maybe you'd want to talk some more about it—help get the feelings out."

Dan remained silent. Where could he possibly begin? A volcanic eruption, that's what she was asking for. There were a hundred questions to ask, but he was afraid of the answers.

"We realize now that we should have shared all this with you. You can't help but have worried, we've been so anxious ourselves. At first we just weren't sure that any of Brian's family *did* have Huntington's disease. We certainly didn't want to worry you, and even after we found out, it seemed pointless—to Brian, anyway. He said you'd feel so helpless."

Dan felt salty tears at the back of his throat. He blinked and continued staring at the light fixture.

His mother stopped talking and waited. "I wish you'd say something to me," she pleaded finally. "It's not going to help to keep it bottled up."

The more she begged him, the less he felt like talking. He hated this about himself. It was as though there was a clamp on his lips, his tongue.

Mrs. Roberts gave a sardonic laugh. "I've been something of a basket case myself—all this planning, this research, this trip—I wanted our family to have one really great trip we could look back on, in case next year, or the year after. . . . Well, I wanted us to go while we had the money, before I start summer school, in case I have to go back to work or something. Your father says that the way I've been rushing around giving orders is making everybody nervous, and I guess he's right. And of course it's not a certainty at all, especially for you." She leaned toward him, her green eyes soft. "Dad explained all that, didn't he?"

"Yes." Dan was glad that he had finally managed to say something. Even one word spoken made it easier.

"If Brian doesn't even have the defective gene, you can't get it at all. So for all we know, you might at this very moment have a one hundred percent certainty of never having it. And all this worry will be for nothing."

"But we *don't* know."

She reached over and lightly caressed his shoulder. "That's right. We don't know."

The salty taste in the throat again, the sting in the nostrils. But somehow, lying back kept the tears from running down his face, and it had been a long time since he'd cried.

"How do people know for sure when they've got it?" he asked. His nose sounded clogged.

"Different ways. Some appear to be agitated or restless. They might begin to jerk or twitch and make strange movements, which they can't prevent, with their arms and legs. Sometimes it's a personality change—a person becomes angry over little things or he can't remember, doesn't keep up his responsibilities. Of course, we all behave like this occasionally, so I guess you don't really know right away—only after the changes continue for a while and begin to get worse . . . until it's obvious to the rest of the family that something's wrong."

"Is that all? A guy just acts sort of drunk or crazy?"

"At first. But as the years go on, the symptoms get worse. It may become difficult for a person to write or talk or walk. His body weakens, and he may die of pneumonia or heart disease or something." She paused. "I'm dumping all this on you at once, Dan. I realize that. I just don't know how else to do it."

He rolled over suddenly and covered his head with his arms, his face in the pillow, letting the tears come. He cried silently, pausing now and then to open his mouth and breathe. It was an enormous relief. He wasn't sure why.

Her hand moved up to his cheek and stroked it, and he let her.

"Do you know about Woody Guthrie, Dan?"

He shook his head.

"He was a famous folk singer. He wrote 'This Land Is Your Land'—you know that song. And his son, Arlo?"

Dan turned his head to one side. "Arlo Guthrie? That was his son?"

"Yes. Woody had Huntington's disease, and nobody knew it at first. His wife noticed that he was walking a little lopsided, and then his speech became slurred. When he flew into a terrible rage one day, she knew that something was really wrong, but the doctors thought he was an alcoholic. Finally a young doctor diagnosed it. Woody lived thirteen years after that, and his wife did a lot to help people understand the disease."

"Then Arlo Guthrie could get it?"

"Yes. Woody had five children, and two of them have it. The others don't know yet."

Dan took a deep breath, held it, and slowly let it out. All the concerts Arlo Guthrie had given, all the places he had gone. He wasn't just lying around waiting for it to happen. Still, in the middle of the night, wasn't he scared?

"That's why I'm researching Brian's family. At first, it was because we needed to know if other relatives had the disease. Now that we know they did, I want to find out as much as I can, clear up a lot of reputations." She laughed a little. "It's become an obsession with me. Nobody understood Brian's family, you know. Your grandmother thought that her husband had been drinking in his later years. She thought that his brother was mentally ill. Brian was ashamed of both his father and his uncle, and it was all so unnecessary. I keep finding references to other relatives' symptoms—things people mentioned only reluctantly in letters. I don't want us to live all secret and shut away, even if Brian is found to have it. I feel like Mrs. Guthrie did—I want people to know and understand."

"One of the Welles sisters has it, doesn't she? Joe said that she was sick."

"Yes. Everyone around here seems to know them —and avoids them. Pearl Welles developed the disease when she was only twenty, which is rather unusual. It's something strange and scary to the country folk."

"And there's no cure, right?"

"Not yet—only medicines to control some of the symptoms. Scientists are working on it all the time, though, and who knows? Maybe in twenty years, by the time you're thirty-five, they'll have a cure. Maybe it will be nothing more than a pill you take every day for the rest of your life—like diabetes or something. Why, you could spend all your time worrying about this and get run over by a truck or something. Nobody knows what will really happen to him in the end."

"Yeah, you're right." Dan sat up and smiled a little. "So bring on the truck!" He felt hungry suddenly. Relieved. They weren't divorcing, they weren't dying—at least not yet. They weren't even spies here in England on an espionage mission. Maybe he'd tell them this at dinner—get a good laugh. It would be nice to see his father laugh.

He reached for his shoes. "I'm starving. I mean, I'm *really* hungry!"

"That's a good sign," said his mother, and she hugged him tightly. "Steak tonight," she added. "We've already decided. Come on in after you've cleaned up a little."

There was a letter waiting for him at the desk as they went out. It was from Bill, on the school paper:

Dear Dan:
Lots of news from the old home town. The Tattler *won second place in the regional competiton and top honors in editorials and photography. Great, huh? Mr. Krause announced the new editorial staff for next year, and "yours truly" got editor-in-chief. I was pretty surprised myself. You made features' editor and Wally's doing news. We had our first staff meeting yesterday, and Krause suggested a series on students' travel experiences. Why don't you lead it off with a feature article on England? Take any angle you want. If it's good enough, we'll give you a whole page, starting with the first issue next September. . . .*

It felt good to be involved again, good to have an assignment. He wasn't going to sit around worrying about something that might never be. A lot could happen in twenty years. For him, at least. Not necessarily for his father.

THE SUN WAS BRIGHTER than Dan had seen it yet in the British Isles. It dazzled the eye, reflecting off the windshield wipers, and finally caused Joe Stanton to reach into his coat pocket for his dark glasses.

Dan looked forward to seeing the gypsies again. This time, he felt, he could view them with perspective. Now that the personal question was out in the open where he could face it, it did not seem as threatening, and he might find that the fears he had experienced earlier had disappeared. When one thing looks spooky, everything seems spooked.

"We won't have much time to stay, Dan," Joe told him. "I've got to pick up some passengers at the station at two and show them around a bit. But it's luck you saw the Faws at all. It's not often you see their *vardos* on the lanes anymore—they're one of a dying breed."

Everyone's dying, Dan thought philosophically. What was it his history teacher had written on the board last semester, something that a man named Manilius had written in the first century? *As soon as we are born we begin to die, and the end depends upon the beginning.* Maybe he should use that quote to begin his article for the school paper, to show how civilizations, once glorious, died out.

"What will happen to the family when Ambrose is gone?" he asked.

"Jasper will probably take over if he's able. If not Jasper, then Orlenda's husband when she marries. A man usually goes to live with his wife's clan—it's the Romany way."

"What's the matter with Jasper? Nat says he's a mute."

"He's no mute."

Dan glanced over at Joe. "You've heard him talk?"

"I've heard him sing."

"Then why. . . ?"

"I don't know. He hasn't spoken since he was a small lad—a *chavvy*. Rose says it came about once after he was *trashed*—frightened, you see. But no one knows what it was that scared him. Whatever it was must have been a great shock to him. It's not his intelligence. He's fit as any man, I'll wager. Shoes the horses, repairs the wagons, plays the fiddle . . . and yet he doesn't talk. But I've heard him off in the woods, away from camp, singing. Not like any other singing, either—a chant, some might call it. A strange mixture of Celtic and Romany—the words all of a muddle. But the man has a voice. Just keeps it to himself. 'Mute Jasper' the gypsies call him, or *ruileah-fein*, meaning madman. They've heard him singing, too, some of them, but they never speak of it. Gypsies don't like to talk about things they can't understand."

"What do you think it was, Joe, that frightened him?"

"I'd be afraid to guess."

"Are you superstitious?"

Joe smiled. "Cautious. A better word."

They turned onto the country lane where the Faws had been two days before, and as they rounded the bend, Dan strained to see the first glimpse of the red and green *vardo*.

"It's gone, Joe!" he said suddenly.

Joe was unperturbed. "They've not gone far, then."

He pulled the cab off onto the shoulder and got out, jumping across the ditch to where the campfire had been. He kicked at the ashes and then held his hands over them.

"They must have left yesterday," he said. "They've only moved on. Not supposed to stay in a camp more than two days, you see, or a *gavver* comes by and tells them to move on."

"A what?"

"A policeman."

"How will we know where they've gone?"

"We'll look about a bit."

The cab moved on down the lane until it came to a fork in the road, and Joe got out once more, motioning Dan to follow. There by the side of the road lay two sticks in the form of a cross, but the sheath of one stick was much longer and pointed toward the narrower lane on the right. Unless one were looking for it, it would have been passed by. Now, examining it closely, it was obviously placed there and secured by human hands.

"It's their *patrin*," Joe explained, "their marker that they leave when they move on." He looked at it again. "So they went that way, then. I would have thought they'd taken the road to Pickering."

They drove slowly through the hilly countryside, the lane growing rougher and steeper until it became a mere byway, and finally it was nothing more than tracks in the heather. There, hidden by a thick grove of trees, stood the red and green *vardo* and, off to one side, a slanted tarp forming a makeshift shelter.

Joe sat for a moment, staring at the tent, and murmured something under his breath that Dan did not understand. But Dan could sense that something was wrong. It hung over the entire encampment—an invisible, noiseless specter. The dogs lay about the fire, resting their heads on their paws. They neither barked nor got up when Joe and Dan approached.

It was then that Dan noticed a form lying under the tarp, with Rose at the bedside. Mrs. Faw stood up and came over to the car.

"It's Mother," she said, and pointed to her abdomen. "The pain is right here. Two weeks it comes, goes away, comes again, but now it never stops. Since yesterday it's worse. I've given her bettony and chamomile, but it's no good. This morning she asked for her best clothes . . ." Here Rose's eyes filled with tears, "and we put her in the tent."

"Do you want me to see her?" Joe asked.

Rose lowered her head, leaving the decision to

him, so Joe got out of the car and went under the tarp. Dan stood awkwardly by the fire, hands behind his back. He could see the old granny in a dress of yellow and black, thin and small, lying on a brightly colored blanket on a bed of bracken. It looked as though everything that belonged to her had been placed close at hand. There were dresses, all in a heap on the ground, slippers, an ornately carved chest, a bird cage, a chair with a velvet pillow seat. . . . Ambrose sat off to one side, arms resting on his knees, his face sober.

Rachel, the young child, squatted by the fire in her grandmother's place, her arms around a dog. Jasper moved back and forth in the shadows at the edge of the camp, going about his morning tasks in a kind of slow motion. Dan waited for Joe, avoiding Jasper's eyes. Whenever he looked, their eyes met. He promised himself he would look at Jasper no more, but again his eyes would seek him out, and always, Jasper was watching. The uneasiness Dan had felt before returned. He was not immune to fear after all, he discovered.

It was a long time before Joe came out from under the tent again with Rose and Ambrose. "It could be appendicitis," he said. "Let me drive her to the hospital. We can move her carefully."

A torrent of angry words issued from the frail body there on the bracken. They were Romany words, but Dan could understand their tone if not their meaning.

Rose shook her head. "No, she won't go. If she's to die, she says, it's to be here." She shrugged.

Again Joe was offered something to drink, and again he sat with Ambrose opposite the fire, leaving Dan to himself. Suddenly Nat came out of the *vardo* and, seeing Dan, came over.

"You'll stay for the funeral?" he asked.

"Your grandmother isn't dead."

"She's dying. She will die by tomorrow."

"How do you know that?"

"I know things," Nat said simply. "I know things before they happen. It's a gift." He looked about the camp where people spoke in whispers. "Come on," he said. "Let's walk."

And as though he had listened to every word, Ambrose called from across the fire, "Take the *juckels*, Nat. They've stayed by Granny since last night. They need the run."

Nat made a noise with his lips, and the dogs stood up, looking at him, then toward the tent where the old woman lay. Nat made the sound again and started walking, Dan beside him, and the five dogs followed. It was not until they had gone over the crest of the hill and started down the other side, however, the camp entirely hidden from view, that the dogs began to trot and finally to run on ahead, tracing the tracks of an unseen scent.

They crossed the wide expanse of pasture, then climbed over a stone fence that separated it from the woods beyond. The brilliance of the sun gave way to sudden darkness as the trees enveloped them, and for a moment Dan felt blinded, barely making out Nat in front of him, who led the way. But when his eyes grew accustomed to the shadows, he saw Orlenda up ahead.

SHE WAS GATHERING STICKS and putting them on the pushcart. Her dark hair hung in two long braids, which she wore in front of her shoulders. Orlenda was barefoot, and her red dress came almost to her ankles. She turned when she heard them coming, paused for a moment, and then went on with her work. She was not laughing this time. As Dan grew closer, it seemed as though the darkness of the girl's eyes shadowed half her face.

He stopped and watched her. "I'm sorry about your grandmother," he said finally.

She straightened up, taller than he was, and brushed back the hair from her face. Her nose was long and thin like her father's, with the same spread of the nostrils at the end. On Ambrose, the nose was ugly, but on Orlenda it was different. She said something that could have been "thank you" in Romany, but Dan wasn't sure. Then she placed her bunch of sticks on the cart and went back to filling her yellow apron.

Nat shuffled impatiently, wanting to be off, but Dan felt it would be rude to leave Orlenda now. He ignored the younger boy's tugging at his sleeve.

"Joe wants to take her to the hospital, but she won't go," he said.

There was the faintest flicker of a smile on the

girl's face. "A fine time she would give the doctors, too," she said. "No, she won't go because she knows she's going to die tonight. She sees things, you know. She told us so herself."

Dan glanced sideways at Nat. Conveniently the boy had taken off and was running down to a stream where the dogs were drinking.

"She wants to go," Orlenda continued, dropping her apronful of sticks on the heap and then leaning against the wagon. "It's her time. What's happening now is only a dream. Her real life begins when she dies. That's what we believe."

Dan watched Orlenda. If it were only a dream, why bother with firewood? With eating?

"We still get hungry," he argued quietly. "We get sick, we even go to sleep and dream."

She laughed a little then, but her eyes were still dark. "Of course. A dream within a dream. But when you dream, you are closer to the real life than when you are awake."

Dan was not sure he understood anything at all, except that the old grandmother was ready to die and wished it so.

"Come on, Dan!" Nat was yelling. "I've found some fish."

"Well," Dan said to Orlenda, "maybe I'll see you again."

"Perhaps you will come to the funeral," she said, and turned away.

Dan jogged down the path to the stream. It was

a wide brook, and the water splashed noisily over the rocks. Nat was standing in water up to his knees and was holding a fish in his hands, waiting for the flipping and flopping to subside.

"You've caught one already?" Dan asked in amazement.

"They come to me," said Nat. "It's a gift."

Dan laughed. "You've a gift for everything."

"It's true."

"Maybe."

"I can tell you when you'll die," the boy said flippantly. "Do you want me to?"

"No," said Dan, and wondered later if he had been afraid.

Nat took off his shirt and tied the fish up in it. Then he slung it over his shoulder like a pack. Every so often the pack jumped, but finally the flapping grew weaker, and at last the fish was still.

There was something decidedly lonely about the fish in the shirt and equally lonely about Nat.

"Stay and eat with us, and I'll cook the fish," he said.

"I don't think I can, Nat."

"I'll give it all to you. It will be Dan's fish," the boy coaxed.

"I have to leave with Joe. He has to pick up some passengers."

"You'll come back?"

"If I can. I don't know how long you'll be here."

"Until the funeral is over. We'll bury her up

there." Nat pointed to a hill half hidden beyond the trees.

"If she dies," said Dan. "What if she gets better and you move on?"

"She'll die," said Nat.

They ambled on down the creek then, Nat, barefoot, along the bed of the stream, and Dan following on the bank beside. Sometimes the distance between them closed until they were almost side by side, other times Nat would go sloshing off to see what the dogs had found farther upstream, and the space between them would grow.

The sunlight fell through a small opening in the trees above and played on Dan's face, like a strobe light—now here, now gone again—and the sound of the water and the patterns of light and darkness seemed to be affecting his senses. He knew he should be getting back to camp, and yet he didn't turn.

Suddenly he heard the singing. He could not tell from which direction it came, for at first it seemed all around him, coming at him from the sky, the earth, the trees, the stream. . . .

He stopped, listening, wondering if Nat heard it, too. It was a young man's voice and, just as Joe had said, more of a chant than a song. The words, if there were words, were strange to Dan's ear, and now and then the music stopped as suddenly as it had begun, as though listening for an answer. Only when Dan was sure it was over did it begin again.

He walked on faster until he was abreast of Nat.

"Listen, Nat," he said. "What is that? Do you hear it? The singing?"

Nat went on, swinging his shirt in his hand without answering.

"Nat?" Dan asked again, and moved this time so that he could see his face. "Don't you hear it?"

Nat stopped, whistled to the dogs, and turned in the water, retracing his steps. "No," he said. "I hear nothing."

They returned to the camp, and once more the dogs slunk over to the fire and lay with their heads on their paws, following the comings and goings with their eyes only. Jasper had obviously beat them back because he was there beside Ambrose, putting the newly mended pots and pans into the back of the cab. Dan stared at him intently, but this time he did not return the look.

"Come tomorrow," Ambrose told them.

"You're sure, then?" said Joe.

"Yes, I'm sure."

"And bring Dan," added Nat. "He can come, can't he?"

Joe looked at Ambrose, and the gypsy's fierce eyes settled on Dan. "Yes, he can come. For a proper Romany funeral, there should be friends."

Joe went back under the tarp once more and said something to the old woman, but this time there was no response beyond a slight wave of a feeble hand.

A few minutes later the cab was making its way along the deep ruts in the pasture to the narrow dirt lane, and finally to the country road where Joe had seen the *patrin*.

For a long time they did not speak. The brilliance of the sun had given way at last to an overcast sky, and there was a decided chill in the air. Joe rolled up the window on his side.

"Did it bother you, Dan?" he asked.

"Some. All that talk about a funeral before she's even dead."

Joe nodded.

"I don't understand them," Dan added.

"Do you understand yourself?"

It was a strange question. Dan glanced over at Joe quickly, but the older man's eyes were on the road.

"No," Dan told him, "I don't understand myself. I don't understand the Faws, I don't understand feelings, I don't understand life. . . . You name it, I don't understand it."

They both laughed a little, but it was a cautious laughter.

"I heard the singing," Dan said, "when I was off in the woods with Nat. I'm sure it was Jasper."

Joe lifted one hand off the steering wheel as if in surprise, then clasped it again. "No," he said, "it couldn't have been Jasper. He didn't leave the camp."

"I heard him! It was just as you said—a young man singing—a chant, really, and the words were strange."

"Did you see him?"

"No."

"Jasper was there all the time I was talking to Ambrose, Dan. He was never out of my sight."

Dan leaned back against the seat and closed his eyes. His forehead felt damp, as if he had been bathed in a cold sweat. "I think I'm going mad, Joe."

"No, I don't think so."

"But I heard somebody singing! If it wasn't Jasper, who was it?"

"I think there are others. I've long suspected it."

"Other what?"

Joe shook his head. "I couldn't even guess."

It was no comfort to know that they were both madmen.

"Listen, Joe, I've got to tell you something else. I saw something the other day—in the Ouse."

Did he imagine it, Dan wondered, or did Joe's face suddenly pale?

"I was down at the river, writing in my notebook, and I saw a fish in the water. I crept over to get a closer look. . . ." He was conscious of the cab slowing down, and he looked out to see if there was an animal on the road, perhaps. But there was nothing. He looked back at Joe and noticed that the man's jaw was tense and stiff. He hesitated, then went on: "At first, when I looked in the water, I saw only a muddy reflection of myself, but suddenly . . . I . . . I saw the head of a Roman soldier, as clear as anything."

Joe bolted back against the seat as though someone had kicked him in the stomach.

"Joe!" Dan said quickly.

The cab weaved to one side and then slowly inched forward again. Joe was visibly shaken.

"What is it, Joe?" Dan questioned. "Have you seen the soldier, too? Is it some kind of hallucination?"

"I've seen it too, and it's no hallucination." The color gradually returned to Joe's face, but he looked older—tired. "Eight years ago it happened, just as it did to you. I was looking down into the Ouse at my own reflection, and I saw that I had on the helmet and breastplate of a soldier. I was so unnerved by the sight of it that I didn't go near the river again for several months. I thought it was my mind, you know —that I was getting a bit dotty.

"Then it was that the Martindale chap spilled the story of what he had seen in the cellar of the Treasurer's House twenty years before. For twenty years he had kept it locked inside himself, just as the old curator had done—just as I was doing, for fear that nobody would understand him. Well, some folks did and some folks didn't. . . ."

"Did you ever talk to Martindale about it?"

Joe shook his head. "I had no need. It was enough for me to know that the ghosts are about, and that it wasn't a trick of the mind. So I went back to the water one day when I was feeling strong, to test what was what, and this time the soldier, he steps up right out of the water—like I'd invited him, you know—the image of myself, and we were joined by others. I fell

in with them, and we marched for a time. The landscape changed. It was still York, I could tell, but a
York of long ago. When the soldiers left me again, I
was there on the bank where I'd first seen them.

"From then on, it was as though I had unlocked
the mind's door. Five or six times it's happened since,
like a story that's unraveling bit by bit. Each time I
feel compelled to join them—I've a great need to
know how it all comes out."

He gave a deep sigh that shook his chest. "It's a
mystery to me why you've seen them too, a lad from
out of the country, even! And yet . . . when I saw you
there in York Station the very first day, I wondered if
you were the one. . . ."

"What do you mean?"

"Six months ago, when the Faws were along this
way, I took a meal with them as always; and afterwards, talking about the fire a bit, the granny read
my fortune. She likes to do it, you see—keeps her in
practice, though it's Rose who does the *duckering* now.
'Twas the last fortune the old woman would read for
me, as it turned out, and it was a strange one. A
young buck, she said, would come into my life and
change it for either good or ill. I tried to get her to
tell me more, half-believing, but she said there was
nothing more to tell, that it would all come about in
its time. I didn't think much more about it then—told
it to my missus, and we had a bit of a laugh over it.
And then I saw you at the station, and remembered."

"Is that why you took me with you to the Faws?"

Dan asked. "To show me to the grandmother, to see if I was the one?"

"Perhaps. I didn't really think it out—just seemed like a good idea at the time—a young lad like you on holiday without much place to go. And it's not everyday you see the gypsies."

"And did she recognize me?"

"If she did, she gave no sign. Today, when I went in to sit by her bed, I asked her about you, but her mind wandered off and she made no reply. But it wasn't just her reaction I was curious about, it was Ambrose's. Because if our fortunes are the same, you see, I wondered if he, too, wasn't looking for the young buck that would change his life; and I believe now that he is. The way he stares at you, it's hard to know if you're welcome or not. One minute he seems to resent your coming, the next he wants you to stay. It's bad business sometimes to bank your life on a fortune. But what is real and what is not? When you have heard voices, as I have heard, and seen faces, as I have seen. . . ."

Dan hunched down in his seat, not wanting to hear more, not wanting to be responsible for any-body's life but his own. That was worry enough. The tension of the day had sapped his strength, and he felt suddenly exhausted, unable to deal with anything else.

"I don't think I'm about to affect anybody's life, yours or Ambrose's," he said, and it seemed an effort to move his lips. "We'll be leaving in a couple days."

"Aye, and it's best you forget all about it, then. You'll not likely see the soldier again."

Dan looked at him. "But you will?"

There was no answer.

"MR. STANTON is such a nice man."

They were walking through the Museum Gardens later that afternoon when Dan's mother said it; they had stopped to study the Multangular Tower that sat back among the trees.

"It's great the way he's been taking Dan around," said Mr. Roberts. "Mrs. Harrison tells me that he gives historical tours of the area. Knows every Roman stone, every medieval arch. . . ." He turned to his son. "If you need any information at all for your essay, Dan, I'm sure he could help you. How's it going?"

"Ten pages so far. No problem."

Ever since Dan had come to York, he had avoided the Multangular Tower. He knew it was there, had read about it in the guide books and seen it from a distance as he jogged by every morning on the wall. He had roamed across the grounds of the public library, where he could see inside the Tower; but he had not gone near it. And he didn't know why.

On this day, because his parents wanted to walk in the garden, he had not been able to avoid it, but he was filled with a dread he could not explain. The dread frightened him more than the Tower itself. He reasoned that it was only the events of the morning, the fatigue, the conversation with Joe that was upsetting him. But now, as he stood off from the Tower staring at the stonework, the dread stalked him again, a dread somehow associated with antiquity.

It was the same fear he felt each morning when, as he jogged, he crossed the Ouse, when he passed the Tower, even along certain sections of the wall where the Roman wall, beneath, was still standing. It was the same strange mixture of fear and attraction that he had experienced the day he peered through the iron grillwork of the Treasurer's House. He had not known what was down there, only that it was a place the Romans had been. As for the Tower, there was nothing to see but stone, yet it was stone that the legionaries had touched. There was something about being here, something about this place, something about his own precarious situation—the collision of past ancestors and future plans—that compelled him to search deeper, even beyond his will. And it was this that frightened him.

It was the same way with the old grandmother's funeral. Dan knew he would go, even though he dreaded it.

"We have only two days left, Dan," his mother said as they walked back to the hotel. "We thought we'd go to the coast tomorrow and visit Scarborough."

"I can't," said Dan, wondering how he would explain it.

Mrs. Roberts looked at him strangely. "Why not?"

"Joe's taking me back to see the gypsies. They'll be moving on after that."

"But . . . we've come all the way to England, Dan, and have seen so little of it, really."

"I promised," said Dan. "They're expecting me."

"Let him go, Ruth," his father said amicably. "Life's too short to spend it doing what other people want you to do all the time. He'll be perfectly okay here with Joe while we're gone."

"Well, all right." Mrs. Roberts squeezed her husband's arm. "It will just be our little trip then. And when we get back, we'll all compare notes on what we did and what we saw. I guess the three of us don't have to stick together like glue, do we?"

So why couldn't he be happy about it? Dan wondered. Why couldn't he be glad they had released him, let him go?

He sat at the small table in his room that night, looking out at the dark sky, listening to the patter of rain on the glass, and added another page to his essay, his mind supercharged by the subject. He felt infected by history, sick, almost, with the intensity of it:

No one knows what happened to the Ninth Legion that was originally stationed here. Some believe that it met with an ignoble defeat and was recalled to Rome. Others believe that the Legion was completely annihilated by the Brigantes. Whichever the case, the Hispana mysteriously disappeared from all record. . . .

Suddenly Dan felt intense cold, as though a door or a window had been opened and a draft was upon him. The air was clammy, and he put down his pencil, shivering. The room seemed to come alive with shadows—some tall, some short, bobbing up and down on the walls, like the shadows of soldiers approaching on horseback.

He leaped up, knocking over his chair, and backed up against the wall, watching the shadows opposite him. Somewhere off in the distance he could hear the sound of marching footsteps, feel the vibration through the soles of his feet. And then he saw that the shadows were getting no taller, were receding, in fact, and that what he mistook for footsteps was the beating of his own heart.

5

HE COULD NOT RETURN to Pennsylvania like this.

He could not leave knowing that he had been felled by shadows alone.

Unlike the disease that stalked his future, this fear he could face now, boldly, and let come what may. Was it better to wait twenty years for a killer that might or might not come than to actively seek out an enemy and have done with it?

As he slipped on his hooded jacket and softly opened the door of his room, he knew exactly what he would do: the thing he feared most. He would go to the Tower, stand inside, and call out the name of Vespasian.

It was strange how any action at all seemed preferable to none. The act of stealing softly down the stairs, of slipping out the side door of the hotel into the alley, and of heading toward the wall seemed to calm him. He wondered if this was the way he would have felt had he been a young legionary in Eboracum, always on the lookout for the Brigantes, or a young tribesman, off on the moors, waiting for a Roman galley to sail up the river from the sea? As a citizen of Eoforwic or Jorwik, would he have felt a certain ironic relief at the sight of pirates and raiders, knowing that at least what he feared the most had come about, that he would have to wait no longer?

The rain came down steadily, almost noiselessly, except when a gust of wind drove it more fiercely against the window panes of the shops that bordered the sidewalk. Here and there a light shone in the darkness, blurred behind the blanket of rain.

Dan knew that the steps to the wall were chained at dusk and that no one was permitted to walk up there after dark. He would surely attract attention to himself if he tried. In fact, at this hour, alone in the rain, he might well be questioned anyway.

He decided to stay outside the wall, to head west past the railroad station and reach Lendal Bridge and the gardens beyond from there. A traveler hiking in from the station seemed more plausible somehow.

On his right loomed the wall, paralleling the road. Strange to think that at one time it offered safety to those inside—in the days before there were cannons or muskets or planes or missiles. Was it better to have lived when war was more personal and less devastating—when there was a bounty on every human head, severed or not, adult or child? Or was it

94

better to live in an age when the enemy had nothing against you personally but could blow your entire town off the map?

It was not a question easily answered. Fear was fear and pain was pain and dead was dead, regardless. Back then there were places to hide, forests to which you could escape, other villages that would take you in. It was disease you could not escape. The Black Plague alone killed over a third of the population of Britain. Dan remembered the day his history teacher had said that to the class: "*A third of the population of Britain!*" he'd repeated. "Think of it!"

Why was it that the more advanced a civilization became in conquering sickness, the more expert it became in the destruction of human life? Was there ever a golden age, anywhere, where science was advanced and men were humane? Were the two incompatible somehow? If a cure were ever found for Huntington's disease, for example, by that time would it really matter?

Despite his attempt to keep his mind occupied with other things, to approach the Tower boldly and determinedly, Dan felt the first sickening wave of dread as he neared the river. He had thought that by coming in from a new direction, he might break the pattern, thwart it somehow. As he stepped onto Museum Street, however, the wind hit him full in the face, as though warning him to keep back, and the dread, like ice water, went coursing through his veins, solidifying his joints, his muscles, his tendons. By the time he reached the bridge itself, his feet were so heavy, his legs so leaden, that he leaned against the rail, grasping it tightly with one hand.

He had felt so courageous back in his room. He had been so convinced that what he was about to do was the best possible thing—that it must be done swiftly and without hesitation—that he had felt in control of himself for the first time since coming to York. But now, as he walked woodenly across the bridge, deliberately setting one foot in front of the other, the plan itself seemed madness. He was inviting his unseen foes to come to him, and he didn't even know what or who they were.

He thought of the comfortable rooms back in the hotel, the soft footsteps of the porters, the secure smell of old chairs and musty carpet, of his parents sleeping unaware. . . . He wished that he had written something in his notebook, given some hint as to where he was going, of what he was going to do, so that, in case. . . .

He had raged inwardly against his parents for keeping their problems and worries to themselves, for not sharing with him. And yet, not once since he had felt the dread had he told them about it—the singing in the woods, the face in the water—all of this he had kept from them.

It was no matter now. There was no turning back. Dan knew that, if he did, the dread would only go with him, to surface again another day. He would go back home with the knowledge that something sinister and terrible had crept into his being in York, and that he had done nothing to exorcise it. He stepped quickly off the end of the bridge and headed for the gardens on the other side.

Once the west corner of the old Roman fort, the Multangular Tower sat heavy and squat among the trees. The slits of windows were invisible now against the dark sky, and the opening, through which he would walk, was like a darker mouth in an already shadowed face.

The dread was like poison in his system. Dan felt dizzy and somewhat nauseated. The blood pulsed so strongly in his temples that he touched his eyes, certain that they were bulging from their sockets. In sixty seconds it could all be over. In less than a minute he could walk into the Tower and call out the name of the Emperor. What would happen then would not be up to him. He would have no more decisions to make, no more barriers to cross. He would have done the thing he feared the most and done it well.

Step by step, as if he were walking on unsure ground, he pressed forward and the opening in the Tower became larger, darker still. Standing just outside the structure, a whiff of its dankness, of moss on old stones, rushed out at him, and he felt as he had outside the cellar in the Treasurer's House. Thirty seconds, fifteen, even . . . it would be done. *Go. Go now. . . .*

Propelled forward by the sheer terror of it, Dan lunged through the opening in the Tower walls and to the very center of the place. He could see nothing in the blackness, only the dark mottled sky in the opening above. He started to yell, but no sound came from his throat because his breath seemed to have been taken from him. Slowly he filled his lungs with air and then, in a half cry, lifted his head and shouted, "Ves-pas—"

A hand clamped suddenly over his mouth, a hand of such power that the fingers seemed forged of steel. Another clasped his arm, whirling him about, and as Dan's eyes searched the darkness, he found himself caught in the grasp of Ambrose Faw.

EACH SEEMED TO SENSE the relief of the other. Dan felt the large hand on his arm relax, but it didn't release him completely. Ambrose swore and shoved Dan roughly up against the interior wall.

"A *mad*man, 'tis what you are," he said, and then let go. He was dressed in several layers of jackets and wore a hat over his wild gray-black hair, which was dripping rain. "Trying to put the *gavvers* on me? Is that what you're about?"

Dan slumped back and let his body slide down the wall until he was sitting on his heels, exhausted. He felt he could not physically answer, and nothing he could say would make sense to Ambrose. The gypsy, however, squatted down beside him and nudged him sharply again. "*Is* it?" he insisted.

"I didn't know you were here," Dan said finally.

Ambrose studied him a moment or two, grunted,

looked up to see from which direction the rain was coming and then, satisfied that they had chosen the most sheltered wall, settled down on his haunches beside Dan, tipping his hat so that the water would run off one side.

"What are you doing here?" he asked.

"I was about to ask you the same thing. Joe said you never came into town anymore."

"And I wouldn't, if it hadn't been for the old woman," Ambrose told him. " 'Twas something I promised her once, that when she was buried it would be with a piece of sod on her breast from the very spot she entered the world. It's a Romany custom, you know, to go with a piece of sod, and if you know the spot where you were born, and if someone fetches a bit of that, it makes the way easier for you in the next world, gives you something to go by."

"She was born in here?" Dan asked incredulously.

"No, down the gardens apiece. Her mother had been ragging when the pains came on. Old Granny showed me the place once. 'Take a bit of the dirt from there,' she told me, and so I came this night to fetch it. But there are *gavvers* about, and they know my face. When I saw them making their rounds, I hid in here. Then *you* . . ." He turned toward Dan again in disgust.

Whether or not Ambrose was telling the truth, Dan decided, there was no point in not being candid with him. If the gypsy was lying, if he was in York for some other purpose, he was a master at it, and Dan could not hope to compete. The fact was, he was too tired to try. He could just make out the ancient coffins strewned about the floor of the Tower—their tops open, filling with water. He shuddered involuntarily.

"I came because I've been afraid of this place," he said. "I've been afraid of it ever since I came to York—every time I passed it, I felt the fear—I don't know why. Somehow I felt that if I didn't face it before I left for home, it would follow me there. . . ." He paused, waiting for a condescending laugh that never came.

"And the shouting?" Ambrose asked finally.

Dan felt a little foolish. "If there was anything in here waiting for me, I guess I wanted it to know I was ready."

"And bring the *gavvers* upon us both," Ambrose said, shaking his head.

Dan was glad that he had come. It had produced nothing, it turned out, but Ambrose. And yet he had done it. He had survived, and now he wasn't alone. Yesterday, if someone had told him he would be sitting in this Tower about midnight with the infamous gypsy himself, Dan would have bet his very life against it. Yet here he was, and glad for the company.

Ambrose pulled up the collar of his outer jacket and put his arms over his thighs to protect them from the rain. "Young men, I'm thinking, sometimes have what the Romanies call *gum sha lack unick*—it means a genius, a miracle. Or perhaps it's more a curse, a *fetich*. My Jasper's got it—took it from the old granny. You sense things, that's what." He sighed. "But it's no good, having the sensing without the wits now, is it? Jasper was not an easy birthing, you see. Rose, she suffered over him. I listened to her cries that night and went out into a stream to swear an oath. I swore that if the child was born a boy, I would make him a defender, a fighter for the Romany ways. And when he was born at last, it was I myself who dipped him in that same stream and washed him. Because of my oath, I took it upon myself to make him a true Traveler."

Ambrose paused and looked up again to check the slant of the rain, moving his body more to one side. "But it never turned out that way. We found him once, when he was just a wee *chavvy*, cowering out in the woods, hiding beneath a juniper tree. He was pale as parchment, and Rose was afraid he had come across poison berries and eaten of them. But the old granny said no, he'd had a sense of something, and if he could only tell us what, he'd be the better for it. But he never talked again, and I had made a vow I could not keep."

"There's still Nat," Dan offered.

Ambrose grunted and spat through his teeth—then suddenly his iron hand clasped Dan's knee, signaling quiet, and he leaned forward and peered through the opening in the wall.

A beam of light was coming across the museum

grounds, and the gypsy got quickly to his feet, pulling Dan with him. They flattened themselves against the wall just inside the entrance. From the edge of the opening, Dan could see two policemen dressed in raincoats ambling toward the Tower, a flashlight bobbing in the hand of one, talking to each other, bantering, casual. They stopped now and then to shine the light on a clump of bushes or into a line of trees, then came nearer. Dan could hear the squish of their feet on the soggy grass. A circle of light flashed briefly inside the Tower, hung for a moment just above the floor, and then disappeared again. The officers did not come any closer or check out the area inside the door.

After they had moved on, Ambrose waited, watching the path they took, planning his own departure. When they had disappeared from sight, he darted out of the Tower and headed through the trees, Dan behind him.

DAN WAS NOT SURE how Ambrose could find the exact place where the old grandmother had been born. One tree looked like any other to him, and there seemed to be an infinite number of secluded nooks where a gypsy mother, years ago, might have given birth to a daughter. Expertly Ambrose moved about —pausing, turning, measuring distances with his eye until he came to a certain tree and a certain bush and a certain place between them. Kneeling down, he took a knife from his pocket and cut out a portion of turf, perhaps six inches square, wrapped it carefully in his scarf, then tucked it inside his coat. Dan stood by, watching.

"How did you get here?" he asked when Ambrose got up again. "You didn't walk all the way?"

"The pony's tethered back on the green, north of the city. I wouldn't chance riding her into town. She would be the first thing the *gavvers* would take of me." The gypsy started to move on, then stopped and looked intently at Dan. "It's a lone time of the night to be testing your courage, mate. Your father know you're out and about?"

"No."

"At what *ker* are you staying, then?" Ambrose asked, and then, translating for him, "What house, eh?"

"It's a hotel, just beyond Micklegate Bar. And I'm not sure if I can get back in, come to think of it. I came out the side door, but it locked again after me. If I go in the front, looking like this, my folks are sure to hear about it."

"I've an old Traveler's trick," Ambrose said, taking his arm as they walked back up toward the street. "Many's the time I've used it when we were in need of some water. It's a fact, you see, that nobody will stop a Romany from going out of his hotel or shop, but he'll block the door with his body if he sees one coming in." Ambrose chuckled to himself. "So what you do is this: you go around to the side door and knock, and not gently either. They have to hear you, and you want them to come at once, not ring for another porter to answer. So you have to knock as if you'll wake the spirits, and then the one at the desk, he'll worry about all the folks who are sleeping and he'll jump up, mad as a man can be, to go and stop the ruckus. And when he goes around to the side door, you slip in the front. More than once I've walked in the front door of a shop this way for a pail of water and, when the keeper comes back and sees me leaving, not coming, he's glad enough to be rid of me, water and all."

"I'll give it a try," Dan said. He walked south on the road then, and the gypsy went north, clinging to the shadows. When Dan turned to look again, Ambrose was gone.

THE NIGHT PORTER sat behind the desk, the evening newspaper spread out before him, pencil in hand. Every now and then he licked the lead, rubbed it slowly between his finger and thumb, and then— holding it poised a moment or two—made a careful, precise mark on the paper. Sometimes he grinned at what he had done—an idiot grin of triumph— and then the pencil would go back behind his ear, and he would concentrate once more on the crossword.

Dan did not particularly care for the night porter. He was still at the desk each morning when Dan went out early to jog, and every morning he said the same thing: "Eh? Up and about with the dairymen, I see." You would think, Dan mused, that after a week or so of the same remark, he could think of something else.

He had thought of going in the front door and telling the porter that something had fallen out of his window and he had gone outside to retrieve it. But that would not explain the matted hair, the jeans and sneakers that were completely drenched, squishing out water with each step he took. The porter would surely mention anything he saw to Mrs. Harrison tomorrow, and she in turn would say something to Mother. Anyway, Dan liked Ambrose's idea better, so he went around to the side door and knocked loudly. Then, to be sure, he banged again.

By the time he had returned to the front door, he could see the porter's shirttail disappearing around the corner inside, and he went quickly in and up to the second floor. He was leaving a trail of water in his wake, however, so he stopped at the door to the public bath, took off his shoes and socks, and made it down the hall to his room just as the porter came upstairs.

He stood inside his room in the dark, breathing with his mouth open so that he could hear every sound. He heard the porter's footsteps on the squeaky floorboards and knew, when the noise stopped, that he had stopped at the public bath. Then slowly the footsteps came on, like those of a hunter, cautiously pausing outside each door, listening, moving on. At last they turned and went back the other way, and finally Dan heard his footsteps going downstairs.

He turned on the lamp by his bed and stepped out of his jeans, hanging them over his chair. His mother would ask about them the next day. It was uncanny the trivia that caught her attention. And then he remembered that his parents would be leaving early for Scarborough, and she wouldn't have time, probably, to fuss.

He felt a pinprick of remorse when he realized how little of this he had shared with them. It was not that they could not accept his fear. Perhaps, some day, when he had worked it through, he would tell them, but he would not tell them now. They were living in a special kind of terror that took all the energy they could muster. How could they deal with this, too?

Dan sat down on the edge of the bed and rubbed the back of his neck with his hand, trying to massage the tension from it. He was no closer to understanding the dread than he was when he had set out, but he had gone to meet the enemy, whatever it was, and it had not been there. An object feared could be a cowardly thing. The more you trembled, the bolder it became. But when you went to seek it out, it retreated, afraid to be seen in its proper proportions.

But of what proportions was this enemy, this unseen thing? A thing could not be measured until it could be found; it could not be weighed if it had no substance. What kind of victory was it to go out to face the enemy if the enemy never came? The fact that it had not come tonight to meet him did not mean that it would not come tomorrow.

Still, what a strange night it had been. He had confided something in Ambrose, and Ambrose in him. He had told the gypsy about the fear because he had been tired, shaken, and too exhausted to lie. He had not expected him to understand. Fear was not a subject men talked easily about to each other. And yet they had talked. . . .

A huge black bird streaked out of the night and took refuge on the ledge outside the window. Rain dripped from its feathers and it preened itself once or twice with its great beak. Then it turned, its brown eye looking in upon Dan, spread its great wings, and gave a wild shriek. At that moment Dan knew instinctively that the old granny was dead.

6

SHE LAY AS THEY HAD LEFT HER, a small, frail body, almost lost in the ruffles and folds of the black and yellow dress. Her skin, etched with hundreds of tiny lines, pulled tightly over her face, revealing the sharp cheekbones, the gaunt hollows beneath them, and the angular chin—all clearly illuminated by the flickering candles at her head and feet. Her arms had been folded over the piece of sod that lay now on her breast, and her gnarled hands, the thumbs bent and deformed by age, the nails curled under, clutched a pipe and a snuff box.

Joe had parked the cab out on the lane this time to avoid the deep ruts in the meadow, and he and Dan had walked around the thick grove of trees that hid the camp from view. Rose greeted them without tears, but her eyes showed the weariness of a long night. As Joe and Dan sat down in the tent beside her, Orlenda stood up and moved out, seemingly glad for the break. She followed her small sister about the pasture, her eyes on the meadow grass.

Ambrose sat off behind the *vardo,* fashioning a coffin from rough pine boards. He worked slowly, silently, his thoughts masked behind the shaggy brows and the beard that covered his cheeks and chin, spilling down over his chest. On the hill in the distance, Jasper was digging the grave where Nat had said it would be. Nat himself was missing.

The drive out that morning had been a quiet one, respectful of the occasion. Dan had seen his parents off on the bus to Scarborough, then waited on the steps for Joe. They had talked of gypsy wakes and burials, customs and traditions, but for some reason Dan had not told Joe about meeting Ambrose in the Tower. He had started to, several times, but something held him back. Nor did Ambrose, when he stopped work for a while on the coffin and came into the tent to rest, make any reference to the night before.

There was no meat cooking in the pot that morning, no sign that there had been breakfast. Even the dogs had not been fed. They lay as they had lain the day before, with heads on their paws, but raised up expectantly whenever anyone came near the cold ashes.

Rose left the tent once to make tea, and Rachel was given a biscuit with it, but for the others, the fast continued. They would have nothing but drink until the burial. Each time a person left the tent, someone else took that place. Never, if they could help it, Joe had explained to Dan that morning, was one person left alone with the body, for the ghost was almost certainly lingering about.

The burial was being delayed as long as possible in hopes that other Travelers might happen along and follow the *patrin* to the camp. Death was a time for being together, for a meeting of the clans. Nat had been sent on the pony along the road to Aldborough to see if there were any gypsies about, to tell them of the death so that there would be a *ceilidh,* a gathering. If none had come by dusk, however, the old grandmother would be buried. They could not risk having the *gavvers* come with their rules and papers, making a regular fuss.

As the talk went on, Dan became conscious of a strange tension between Ambrose and Joe Stanton. It was such a finely tuned thing, so delicate, so nearly invisible that he almost missed it. And yet it was there. Rose had been talking about the old granny's last few years, and how she had seemed to live in a world of her own, talking to people who were never there, laughing at some hidden joke, as though her soul had long since departed, leaving the body behind.

" 'Tis the way when they get on," Ambrose said, holding his cup in both hands, letting the steam bathe his face. "It's the childhood she's remembering again —the mother, the sisters. . . . Some say if you give an old woman a doll, she'll take it to bed with her like a *chavvy.*"

But Rose was shaking her head. "It never seemed that way with her, Ambrose. She saw things that frightened her, she said—soldiers she told me once —chariots, bothies all afire. . . ."

"She was dreaming then, woman. There was no line between her waking and sleep. I dream such things myself, but I know them to be dreams, though the soldiers are so real sometimes I think they have touched me."

"Perhaps it's neither dream nor reality but something different still," Joe suggested quietly. "Perhaps it's a state where we are neither awake nor asleep, here nor there, but in a different time altogether. . . ."

"*Conya!*" Ambrose spat out the word with such emotion that Dan could guess its meaning. "You talk like a scholar with brains in his feet! A man is born and a man dies, and where he was before or where he goes afterwards is not for us to guess, nor to tamper with. We are either in the ground or above it. To be about with one foot in and one foot out, neither here nor there. . . . Who is to know, then, whether a man he meets on the *drom* is dead or alive, spirit or flesh?"

Why was he so upset? Dan wondered, watching silently. Only the night before he had talked about the miracle or curse that sometimes made young men see things that others could not see. It was as though, applied to Jasper, it was acceptable somehow, but applied to Ambrose and his own dreams, it reached terrifying proportions. Joe said what Dan was think-ing:

"And Jasper? He sees nothing, Ambrose, that we don't see? Hears nothing?"

Rose answered for him: "It is a bit like *duckering*, Joe. The old Granny could take your hand and tell you where you had been and where you would go. I myself can see a bit of the future in a palm, but never had much luck looking for the past. It's a special gift to do both, and perhaps it is so for Jasper. What he sees and what he hears are a bit of the past, a bit of the future, but all the time he is here among us. There is no other place except what the mind in-vents."

"And you're sure, then," Joe continued, "that be-cause you don't see what Jasper is seeing or hear what he hears, it doesn't exist?"

"It does not exist," said Ambrose quickly, anger surfacing again in his voice.

For almost a minute he and Joe Stanton stared into each other's face, eyes intent, mouths set. Dan could not understand the feelings the conversation had evoked. And then, as though on a given signal, the shoulders of both men relaxed, stooped. Ambrose returned to his tea, and Joe withdrew once more into himself.

Morning mingled with afternoon, with nothing to distinguish one from the other. Occasionally there was the soft scraping sound of Ambrose's tools on the pine boards, or a low murmur from Rose followed by an answer from Joe, or, up on the hill, the clink of Jasper's shovel striking a rock.

Dan's body ached with the fatigue of sitting, so he stood up finally and walked slowly about the camp. He was trying to memorize the look of the place, the sounds, the smells, so he could put them all in his article for the school paper. A gypsy burial, that's what he would write about. It would be a fine lead for the series.

Orlenda was kneeling at the edge of the pasture, making a little braid of wild flowers from the blossoms that Rachel was picking and placing in her lap. For a brief moment Dan paused, struck by the familiarity of the scene, certain he had seen it before, had been here before, yet he knew he had not.

"It will be for Granny's hair," Orlenda told Dan when he went up to her. "She always wanted a proper Romany burial, next to the hedgerow of a church, with all of her kin about and a thornbush on her grave. That's the best, you know. But out here...." She looked around. "Well, there's no church...."

There was a sudden crashing and crackling of underbrush in the grove of trees near the lane, and Nat emerged, covered with burrs, his shirt torn.

"*Gavvers,*" he said. "I saw them on the *drom* and hid the *grai*."

Ambrose stood up. "Did they see you, then?"

"I don't think so."

Joe came out of the tent and motioned to Dan.

"Come on. We left the cab on the lane. They're sure to question it."

Dan followed him down the long path that curved around the trees and out to the road. It was too late to move the cab, however. A policeman had parked behind it and was getting out.

Joe tipped his cap as they came down the path. " 'Afternoon, officer."

"Hello, Joe. I thought this was your cab. Getting so I can memorize the license numbers."

"Then you've a better memory than I," Joe said. "I forget them myself." He motioned toward Dan. "I've a lad I'm keeping for a few days and thought we'd seek out the gypsies. Heard the Faws were on their way through and hoped I'd still find them here. Haven't seen their camp about, have you?"

"As a matter of fact, I was checking on them myself," the officer said. "They were on the road a few days back. Wanted to be sure they'd moved on."

"Well, I suppose they could be to Pickering by now," Joe said, and then to Dan, "We could take in a cricket match, instead, eh?"

"Will do the lad more good than a chat with Ambrose Faw." The policeman laughed. "You're corruptin' young minds, Joe, bringing him to the gypsies. You leave your cab out on the road like this when the Faws go by, it'll go along with 'em."

Joe smiled and shook his head. "Never took anything from me that I didn't give them, officer. And that's more than I can say of the gas man and the butcher."

The officer laughed again and got in his squad car. "There's a cricket match at four, Joe—if the rain holds off."

"Obliged," said Joe. They watched the police car round the bend and disappear, and when the sound of the motor had died away, they drove the cab deep into the meadow behind the trees and parked it by the *vardo*.

"YOU'RE ON YOUR WAY TO PICKERING," Joe told Ambrose.

The big gypsy smiled broadly, revealing a gold tooth at one side of his mouth.

Rose was relieved. "Mother will have a proper burial, then, without a coroner asking this and that."

Ambrose turned to Nat. "No sign of the Coopers' *vardo*, then? Nor the Boswells'?"

"I went as far as I could—only tinkers and *mumpers* on the *drom*."

"Did you leave a *patrin?*"

"Yes, and tied a bit of red on it so they'd know of the death." Nat was glad to see Dan and grabbed at his shirt. "Come with me to get the *grai*. I left her in the trees."

Dan, in turn, was relieved to have Nat back in camp. His presence detracted, somewhat, from the somber air. They went out to the road, walking along the shoulder, ready to bolt at the first sound of a car. But the narrow lane stayed empty.

"Who are the *mumpers* and tinkers?" Dan asked, not used to the boy's heavy use of Romany.

"Oh, them!" Nat tossed his head. "Trash, rubbish. *Conya*. They follow the gypsy ways, but there's not a drop of Romany blood in any of them. Tramps, that's what they are."

Dan smiled at this outburst. "Not a trace of Romany blood in me either," he chided.

"You're different. And I'm glad you came, because we'll be leaving right after after the burning."

"The burning?"

"Of the tent and all of Granny's things."

"You *burn* them?"

"Yes, all except the little things she gave us before she died."

"Why? Can't your mother use them?"

Nat looked puzzled at the question. "She would never do that! We burn them so that Granny's spirit will never see anyone else wearing her dresses, or drinking from her cup." He stopped, picked up a flat pebble in the lane, and skipped it down the road as Dan was used to doing with pebbles at the ocean. "Romanies used to burn everything, you know. When a man died, his *vardo* would be burned, his guitar smashed, his *grai* sold, his *juckels* killed—even his grindstone would be rolled into the sea. But. . . ." He shrugged. "We don't have so much any more. Now, when someone is dying, we put him in a tent outside with all his possessions, and after the funeral, we burn the tent, not the *vardo*."

Nat seemed to know instinctively where it was he had hidden the pony and made his way through the gorse and burrs, spreading the underbrush apart with his hands and waiting for Dan to catch up with him.

The piebald pony waited patiently. It was a heavy brown cob with thick flanks and sturdy haunches. Its mane was white, its tail white, and there were shaggy white fetlocks above each hoof. Nat spoke to it gently in Romany, *cushti grai, cushti grai,* stroking its long nose, and the pony nuzzled him under the arm. He held the reins while Dan climbed on, somewhat awkwardly, for there was no saddle or stirrups.

Nat stood looking at Dan before he pulled himself up.

"I still want to trade for your belt," he said, his eyes on the buckle. "If you like, I'll trade only for the clasp."

Dan grinned. "Hey, listen, Nat! I told you. It's the only belt I brought with me."

"You could buy another. I'll pay you for it."

"I've got to hold my pants up."

"I'll give you a rope."

Dan laughed. "No rope. But maybe . . . just before I go. I'll have to think about it."

Nat climbed on ahead of him, and the pony moved slowly through the thick trees toward the camp, making its own trail. Nat let the reins lie loosely about the animal's neck.

"When I die," Nat said determinedly, "there will be no *vardo* to burn, no *grai* to sell. Jasper can have the *vardo.* I'm going to live in a flat with a number on the door and a television set on the table."

"Yeah? When did you decide all that?"

"A long time ago."

"What does your father think about it?"

"We don't talk on that."

Through the trees, Dan could just make out the clearing. Jasper had come down from the hill and was sitting on the grass in his undershirt, his back soaked with sweat. Rose passed out beer, mixing the drink with tea before she gave some to Rachel. Afterwards they sat about in silence, and the afternoon seemed to inch along in slow motion. All movements, all speech, seemed hesitant or delayed, as though the mourners were numbed by cold or listless with heat. People went in and out of the tent, sitting in threes or fours beside the grandmother's body, and the candles continued to burn. Some crossed the meadow to the stream in the woods beyond and came back again, slowly, or trekked up the distant hill where the grave lay waiting. The clouds shifted, the sky darkened, shadows fell in the meadow below sending a chill over the camp. Then, just as suddenly, the clouds moved on again, letting the sunlight through.

It was hypnotic, Dan decided—either that or the drink, yet he did not feel lightheaded. He was in perfect control of his mind and body, and yet he sensed somehow that he was changing—either he or the things around him. It was the silence, he told himself; the flickering of the candles; the slow movements. He shivered, feeling the need to get up, move about. He glanced toward Jasper, who was coming across the meadow, and suddenly his heart seemed trapped in his mouth, for there, in Jasper's place, yet Jasper surely, was a strange-looking man in a coarse reddish shirt, a skin about his loins, his hair stiff with lime.

Dan uttered a cry and half sprang to his feet, one hand on the ground. The strange creature turned to look at him, his face blurred, and he became Jasper once more. Their eyes met, and Dan knew, from the look on the face of the mute, that something had passed between them.

He sank down on the grass again, looking awkwardly about at the others. Faces turned away, shoulders slumped, and eyes focused once more on the old woman in the tent, as though they had witnessed something they should not have seen. All but the eyes of Jasper. No matter where Dan sat or how long he looked away, when he looked back again, Jasper was watching him, and Dan knew that he should never have come to this place.

It did not happen again. Dan sat tensely, heart pounding, eyes darting here and there, watching the movements, the shadows, alert for any sign of danger. The dread he had felt so often before encircled him again like some creature of the sea, squeezing his chest, forcing the breath from his lungs. It had been madness to come here, madness to stay. And yet, as the afternoon wore on and Rachel played in the meadow, the fear gradually lessened, and by five o'clock, he began to suspect the drink. He would take nothing more.

The family began their preparations for the funeral dinner. Jasper grabbed two hens that had been strutting about the *vardo,* one in each hand, and—holding them by their legs—took them far across the meadow where any blood that was spilled in the killing would not desecrate the old granny's wake.

With the death of the chickens, the camp came to life.

"Orlenda, bring the *cosh,*" Rose instructed, and Orlenda went into the woods for the kindling.

When the feathers had been plucked and the meat cut into pieces and placed in the stew pot, Rose took off her apron and washed her hands. Ambrose and Jasper had gone to the stream to clean up and when they returned, they put on the fresh shirts that Rose had laid out for them, turning them inside out for good luck. The dogs, who had eagerly sniffed at the chicken feathers and stood around the kettle a short while before, now sensed the change in mood and slunk back away from the circle. It was time to bury the old woman.

No one touched the body of the grandmother. Holding the ends of the blanket on which she lay, Ambrose and Joe gently lifted the small body and lowered it down into the coffin that Ambrose had made, burying the blanket with her. The lid was nailed in place.

Gently the pine box was lifted to the shoulders of Jasper and his father, and the procession started up the steep hill beyond the meadow. It was a rough climb, for whatever path there had once been was overgrown with gorse and bracken. When they reached the crest where the ground leveled out, the dogs hung back, and one of them made a small whining sound in its throat. A second dog took it up, and then all five dogs were howling. Ambrose spoke sharply to them, and instantly they ceased.

"All we'd need to bring the *gavvers*," he said.

The coffin was placed on the ground, ropes were slipped under both ends, and the grandmother was lowered into the earth. Orlenda, squatting on the edge of the grave, put her head down in her lap, her face in the folds of her red skirt, rocking back and forth on her heels, weeping.

The service was said in Romany. Rose handed a flagon of ale to Ambrose, and he poured it over the coffin. Each member of the family picked up a clod of earth or a spray of heather and dropped it down the hole. Then Jasper took his shovel and began filling in the dirt. Others helped by pushing it in with their hands. When the hole was filled, Ambrose walked over it, tamping it down, and finally Rose planted a small thornbush she had dug up elsewhere and entwined a long piece of red yarn in its branches. The dogs, sensing somehow that it was over, turned and started back to camp.

Food brought about a relaxed and mellowed mood after so long a fasting. Rachel, sitting next to her father, teased him as she held out bits of bread for him to eat and then, when he snapped at them, jerked her hand away, laughing merrily.

Dan had vowed not to eat or drink anything else,

but the fear had left him and his stomach ached for lack of food. He took the stew that was offered but refused the drink.

THERE WAS TALK of burning the tent that evening and moving on. Dusk was beginning to sift down through the trees, and still no other Travelers had arrived.

"The Boswells would have come by now if they'd seen the *patrin,*" Ambrose brooded. "Once we light the tent, we have to be off. Someone will see it or smell of the smoke, and the *gavvers* will be at us."

They fell silent then. No one besides the family had sat with the body as the old grandmother lay for the last time on the bracken—no one, that is, but Dan and Joe Stanton. No one else had walked her to the grave. It did not seem right that they should leave her there unmourned by the many people who had known her over the last eighty-nine years.

So still had they all become, even Rachel, that a magpie, sitting on a branch behind Ambrose, suddenly flew down and alighted in the clearing not far from the cooking pot. The dogs watched it without flinching, ears up, eyes alert.

There was something about the magpie's appearance, Dan noticed, that alarmed the family. Orlenda sat with one hand to her mouth, watching the bird hop even more boldly, first forwards, then back, cocking its head.

Ambrose himself did not move. "There is only one, then?" he asked finally of Orlenda, who sat across from him.

Her eyes moved up to the branch from which the bird had come. "Yes, only one."

And then, as though the magpie had not alarmed them enough, it flew to the top of the *vardo,* and perched there for a moment before flying away.

Ambrose uttered an oath in Romany.

"You know what it means," said Orlenda. "We can't travel till tomorrow."

Again Ambrose swore at the magpie and pounded one fist into the palm of the other.

Rose, however, was more philosophical. "Maybe it's a sign for the best," she offered. "Perhaps the Boswells are on their way, and we'd have missed them if we'd moved on."

Coming from Rose, the official soothsayer, that seemed a reasonable conclusion. Ambrose filled his glass again and sat drinking quietly. Unbidden, Jasper got his fiddle from the *vardo* and began plucking tentatively at the strings. It was difficult to tell where the tuning left off and a song began, but gradually the plucking became a melody. His mother sang the words. It was about a girl in a Galway shawl who went to meet her lover and found him hanged. Rose's voice had a thin, wavery quality to it, as though she were singing through her nose with hardly any breath at all.

Whether it was the music or the lengthening shadows around him, Dan began to feel the first icy tremors of dread again. He did not want to spend the night in this place, and yet he knew that they would. The burial would not be over until the burning of the funeral tent, and that would now be delayed until morning. What the magpie meant, he did not know, but he knew they would not move on this night.

There was a tension still between Joe and Ambrose, which added to his unease. Thinking back, Dan realized that it had always been there. Despite their handclasp, their hug, their drinking together and their toasts, despite Joe's obvious welcome in the camp, there was a distance between the two—imperceptible at first, but there. They were like two dogs that met, nuzzled, went through all the amenities of friendship. And yet, the hair on the back of the neck had bristled, the flanks had quivered, as though each anticipated a clash that never came. Watching them now before the fire, Dan felt it even more strongly.

It made him decide to tell Joe what he had seen that afternoon when he had looked at Jasper, in case both their lives were in danger. What if the magpie meant nothing at all? What if it was merely a ruse to keep them here? Was it possible that they blamed him, somehow, an outsider, for the old grandmother's death?

Dan maneuvered about the circle until he was sitting by Joe's side and waited till Jasper had begun another tune on the fiddle. Then he leaned over.

"Joe, I saw something this afternoon."

He watched Joe's face anxiously, but the man gave no sign of having heard. He whispered again:

"Listen, Joe, I was watching Jasper cross the meadow this afternoon and suddenly he changed. I swear it! He looked like . . . like some primitive thing. . . ."

"Don't *speak* of it again!" Joe said sharply, refusing even to look at him. He got up suddenly and moved away.

Dan felt his pupils expanding in the darkness, his throat blocked by fear. He was afraid he would not be able to breathe, to think. . . . It was like a dream where suddenly everything began falling around him, but his legs wouldn't run.

What did it mean? What was the matter with Joe? Was there anyone in camp he could talk to—Orlenda, even? Nat would barter away Dan's soul, he was sure of it, just for his belt with the eagle buckle.

THEY SLEPT OUT OF DOORS that night. Only Rose and her daughters slept in the wagon. Nat helped Dan gather bracken from the surrounding hills to press down into a kind of mattress and covered it with a blanket. Dan moved mechanically, watching, listening, every nerve in his body waiting, ready to run. Even after he lay down, his body was tense—taut.

The horses stood dozing off by the edge of the trees, heads down; the dogs lay on their sides around the fire; and the hens had gone to roost in the pan box under the *vardo*.

Nat, a few feet away, had gone to sleep easily, naturally, his mind unencumbered with doubts. Joe, Ambrose, and Jasper all lay under a tree opposite the fire, their bodies gray heaps in the darkness, silent, unmoving. The fire had burned down to small pin-points of red among the ashes, like the eyes of an animal, Dan thought, watching from the shadows.

The bracken stuck him through the blanket, and he changed position, keeping his arms under his head so that he could see the whole camp. He would not allow himself to sleep for a minute. And yet, as the night progressed, he could tell that he had been drift-ing in and out of dreams. Each time he awoke, the clouds had shifted dramatically once again.

At first he thought it was a horn out on the lane, but it was not a horn like the one in Joe's cab; he thought of the police and wondered if they were com-ing back. Raising up on one elbow, he looked down the path to the road, then realized that the blast had come from the other direction, the woods. It did not sound again, however, and all was quiet.

He lay back down, his eyes huge in the darkness, listening intently. It was then that he heard the tramp of feet, the rustle of underbrush. He lay stunned, without breathing—sure that the others would hear it, too. But no one spoke. No one stirred. Even the dogs were quiet. Then suddenly he felt a nudge on one leg and, turning, looked up into the face of a Roman soldier.

7

H E HAD MET UP WITH IT at last: the dread, or
the cause of it. He recognized it in the
form of the centurion who now looked
down upon him. His skin felt clammy, as though the
door of a tomb had been opened, and the cold draft
brought with it the smell of death.

The trumpet was silent now, and the other legionaries marched on by, as though oblivious to Dan's
presence. Their footsteps were like muffled drum-
beats; yet the soldiers hardly marched in precision.
They moved dejectedly, heads down, shoulders
slumped, weary and solemn.

Dan had raised himself on his elbows, shivering,
ready to spring, but the passing of the column
stopped him. There were no horses in the unit, only
men, each in need of a wash and a shave. Their kilts,
green in color, seemed to have been handmade, and
the sandals, cross-gartered to the knees, were loose

and floppy. Unlike pictures Dan had seen of Roman soldiers, they carried round shields, and the plumes of their helmets were not the red horsehair crests of the Ninth Legion but rather undyed feathers.

Dan was amazed that he could see the men in such detail in the darkness, as though they were illuminated with a special kind of light. But they did not have the appearance of specters. They were three-dimensional and took up space as surely as Nat, asleep there on the ground.

He was afraid for a moment that they might surround the camp; he wondered if he should wake the others while there was still a chance to escape. But the soldiers went on, following no path, disappearing into the darkness.

"What do you want?" he asked the centurion.

There was, of course, no response. The soldier simply motioned, with a jerk of his spear, for Dan to get up.

Dan hesitated, stalling for time, looking about the camp to see if he could expect help from Ambrose or Joe. One could ambush the soldier from behind, possibly—the other take his spear. . . .

But the others were slumped in the posture of sleep and made no movement. Was it possible that they had not heard, that none of them had seen?

He slowly reached for a boot, and the centurion kicked the side of Dan's leg, impatient to be off. Dan put one boot on, then the other, trying to make as much noise in the process as he could. No one stirred.

Eerily, even the dogs slept on. Gooseflesh rose on his arms.

He was overwhelmed, suddenly, by the feeling that this was a moment of decision—that if he went, he would never return. Terror clutched at him, and yet, inside himself, he realized a fear even more deadly, for he sensed that some part of him wished to go. Some part of him craved an end to uncertainty, with no price too high for the relief of it.

No words had passed between him and the centurion, but the soldier had come for him alone, and he knew it. If he went, he would become one with the past, with the future decided for him. He would be only a number among the legionaries, bound to the centurion, and all he need do thereafter was obey orders. In opting for security, he would lose forever the hope of change.

Suddenly he spun about and bolted. Like a wild man, he leaped over Nat, on across the sleeping dogs and the cold ashes of the fire, running with back bent, as though ducking crossfire—struggling, with every ounce of effort—for the hill beyond.

He dared not go down into the woods to the stream; the soldiers had come from that direction. Nor did he wish to go into the mist of the meadow, where they had disappeared. He thought fleetingly of the lane beyond the trees, where a passing motorist might stop for him, but chose instead the high hill because it was open and exposed. If he were to die this night, in this place, let it be close to the grandmother who had not feared her own death. Let it be on a dark peak next to the sky, grappling one to one with this silent phantom.

The centurion was close behind him, and Dan remembered the man's spear. It would take only a single throw to hit him. The legionaries, he knew, were expert marksmen, and he was a living target silhouetted against the moon, impossible to miss. His back tingled with the awful expectancy of the javelin's tip; his ears strained for the whirring sound of a spear in midair.

But the spear did not come. Gasping and panting, Dan was tempted to turn around, to see how close the soldier was, but he could hear breathing close at his heels and dared not slow for a second. There was nowhere on the hill to hide, no place to seek refuge, and suddenly the centurion lunged. Dan felt a strong hand on the calf of his leg. He yanked his foot free only to feel it secured by the other hand, and he fell to the ground, twisting over on his back.

Instantly the soldier was upon him, the cold metal of his breastplate pressing against Dan's chest. He had thrown down his javelin and unsheathed his dagger, but that, too, he threw down beside him.

Dan's heart leaped in terror. If the soldier did not want his life, what then? His mind? His will? He cried out in panic, struggling to get a hold on his adversary, to push him off, to run again; but where he would run to, he did not know.

The armor on the centurion's shoulders was fitted in vertical strips like the hide of an armadillo, and the curved metal bands that bound his chest were also fitted one over the other, held together in front with leather straps. Dan seized one of the straps, pushing with all his strength, and managed to shove the centurion off to one side, throwing himself on top of him.

The soldier, despite his short height, was by far the stronger and, with all his armor, heavier too. With one muscular arm he grabbed Dan by the throat, pushing him away, gaining the advantage. Dan pummeled fiercely at his attacker, but the blows only made strange clanking noises as they struck the metal.

Somewhere off on Dan's right, a figure moved from out of the darkness and stopped for a moment, watching cautiously. Turning his head, Dan could make out the strange-looking man he had seen earlier, the one with lime-caked hair, and he cried out again, not caring, hoping that someone in the camp had awakened and come to help. But the creature disappeared into the shadows and did not return.

The dagger lay within reach. At one point Dan's hand came as close as an inch to it. One lunge and he would have it. One thrust in the back, beneath the soldier's breastplate, and the fight would be finished. As they rolled there on the ground, the metal actually touched his hand, yet Dan did not pick it up. The opportunity came and went, yet neither of them took it. The dagger remained where it was.

The senselessness of the struggle began to irritate him. It was an exercise in idiocy. Neither of them knew the other. Each belonged to a different time, a different place. What grudge was there? What need of force, of show of strength? Why had the centurion singled him out, and why had he stayed behind alone when all the soldiers together could easily have taken the whole camp? What possible use could Dan be to this man?

His limbs began to ache with weariness. The centurion, too, was tiring. Perspiration dripped from both their faces, mingling together. The air was pungent now with the odor of sweat, of damp leather, and the sharp metallic smell of armor.

The sound of the centurion's breathing had become more human, dulled by fatigue, more typical of a man grown weary of battle. And suddenly Dan realized that he was no longer afraid. It was as though, having resigned his body to what he could not help, his spirit had become the victor.

Sensing the weakness of the other, Dan reached for the leather straps once more to throw the centurion off-balance, to right himself, to call an end to the farce. But when his hand touched the soldier's chest, he felt no armor, no metal strips, no shoulder guards, no straps. The body seemed to have grown suddenly more frail, more gaunt, and—when Dan pushed away and sat up—he found himself staring into the dirt-stained face of Joe Stanton.

THEIR EYES MET as if they were coming together in a fog, the blurred edges growing sharper, faces more distinct. Joe sat breathing heavily, shoulders rising and falling. His head was thrust forward, his eyes fixed and trancelike. His lips moved once but made no sound. He stared at Dan for a long time and finally said:

"So we've had a go at it, eh?"

Dan fell back on the grass, closing his eyes as the blood coursed through his head, swishing in his ears with each pulse beat. He felt exhausted, numb. For a long while he could say nothing at all, and then:

"What was it all about, Joe?"

"I don't know." Joe wiped his damp face on his sleeve and shook his head, running his tongue over his grimy teeth. "So it's come to this," he added, as if to himself.

"What were you trying to do? Choke me? The way you had hold of my throat. . . ."

A look of fear passed over Joe's face. "I wouldn't have hurt you, Dan."

"Then why did you do it?"

Joe shook his head and let it drop over his chest with weariness.

It didn't make sense. They each had taken part in a charade they did not understand.

"Were we sleeping, Joe, when it happened?"

"Not I. When I heard the trumpet, I knew they were coming. I went down to the stream, hoping to head them off, but it didn't work. I fell in step with them, and it was up through the camp we came. . . ."

"What did you want from me?"

Joe looked at him, bewildered. "I don't know,

Dan. I came to this chap on the ground, and I knew I'd need of him, but I didn't know why. And then he started to run. . . ."

"You didn't know it was me?"

"No more than you recognized me. It's all of the past. We took part in a scene that once happened here, that's all I can figure out."

"What do you mean? You think we lived before in another age and went back to relive it again?"

"No, I don't think we went back. It's as though the past came to us, and we were changed for that moment or minute or hour. . . ." He paused. "I became one of the soldiers. That much I know. But of what Legion or what time, I'm not sure. It would appear that it was long after the Ninth Legion disappeared. Other legions had come to take its place; soldiers came and soldiers went, but slowly troops were called back to Rome to fight the Gauls. The men left here were next to forgotten. It was like a small police force supposed to protect the whole province, made up of volunteers and men who married the local women. When they went out on patrol, they went in parties of twenty or more, for fear of ambush. Stayed for a week or a fortnight and came back tired and dirty, like the ones you saw tonight. I think it's one of those patrols we're seeing, same as Martindale saw."

Dan watched him. The moon had come out from behind a cloud again, and there on the top of the hill, unshaded by trees, they were exposed to each other. Dan could read his friend's face as though they were sitting together by a lamp.

"Ghosts, then," Dan said finally. "Is this what we're seeing?"

Joe did not answer directly. "For eight years, ever since this first happened to me, I've studied what people have written about it. A psychic imprint, some call it. Some believe, you see, that when a person is engaged in an extremely emotional experience—as a soldier is in battle—that person leaves a psychic imprint—an event in the atmosphere, which can be seen by a living person. Some say that strong emotions, once experienced, produce lasting effects on the atmosphere—like a moving picture, you know—appearing again and again. Many years later, centuries even, this can be seen or felt by another person with deep feelings about the past—possibly even a sensitive person who is simply going through a crisis of his own. It's as though these scenes are all around us—like electricity in the air. But, like electricity, a conductor is needed, and perhaps people like you and me are the conductors. There is something about us that makes it possible to see an incident that took place a long time ago, become a part of it, even."

"I felt cold before it happened," Dan told him. "Even before I saw the soldier, there was this draft—this morbid fear—a cold, clammy stink. . . ."

"Yes. I know when they're coming by the intense cold—even on a summer day it's happened. Energy, they say, in the form of heat, must be extracted from the atmosphere to enable the ghost or the imprint to be seen and sensed, a sort of electrical discharge in reverse. Just before I heard the trumpet, I sat up, hugging myself with my arms, freezing. And each time it happens, the scene is extended a bit more. Up to now, I have never moved from where I was. If I actually marched with the soldiers, they very considerately put me back where I had been, or perhaps I wandered back of my own accord. But after tonight, after grappling with you, following you, I fear for the next time, for what I might do."

"There won't be a next time, for me anyway. We're leaving York tomorrow."

Joe nodded. "I'm glad of that."

"Why were you so angry this evening when I told you about Jasper, about what I had seen? Why did you tell me not to mention it again? It wasn't like you."

"Because I felt that to talk about such things might bring them upon us tonight, and as it turned out, I was right. I knew you would be leaving soon, and because you had seen a face in the water, I knew that you were susceptible to what I have been experiencing. I wanted you to put it out of your mind."

"What is it about Jasper, do you think? What does he become?"

"I can't tell you, Dan. I've seen it too, the transformation—the wild man with the limed hair—always lingering in the shadows just beyond reach of the legionaries. What he is or why he is, I can't explain. A tribesman, perhaps. That's the best I can do."

They sat for a while, the dampness of the night

earth soaking through their clothes. Now there was no moon again, no stars. Dampness pervaded the air as well.

"Why did you come here?" The question came so suddenly, so unexpectedly, that Dan was taken by surprise.

"Mom told you, Joe. We're on vacation. She's researching Dad's side of the family."

"Why did you really come?"

He had sensed something, then.

"Mother's going to school this summer; it had to be now or not at all," Dan said, dodging the question.

But Joe waited.

Dan chose his words carefully. Was it still a secret —the family history? Was it forever to be regarded as a skeleton in the family closet? He had not resolved it yet—how much he was to tell people.

It was a night, however, for being honest.

"We're one of those families, Joe—those 'magrums' you were telling me about. Mother wanted to find out where it all began. That's why she went to see the Welles sisters. You must have guessed."

"Yes."

"Of course, she didn't find out where it began, because it goes back forever, practically. In fact, it was only a few days ago that I found out about it at all. I hadn't known." He took a deep breath. "I've been pretty upset about it. And now—this. It's wild, isn't it? Perhaps that's why I've seen the ghosts, why it's *possible* for me to see them. I'm a bunch of nerves, that's all. I've got antennae out in all directions. But what about you?"

"I feel I was looking for you, Dan, before you ever came to York, but I don't know why. I thought maybe it was the old Granny's prediction, but that doesn't really explain it. Why do I appear in these scenes as a centurion instead of a Celtic tribesman? Did my ancestors, perhaps, come over with the Hispanic to stay and intermarry? I've sympathy for hero and villain alike, you see, because they change places, depending on which side you're on. I've a feeling for the Brigantes who roamed these hills long before the Roman invasion. It was their land, their people. And I've sympathy for the legionaries sent to protect the villas and the towns and temples that Rome had built in the south. The tribesmen came into battle with offerings to Brigantia, and the Romans to Mithras and Mars. Who's to say who should have been the victor? Let the gods fight it out in heaven, that's what!

"What would you value more, the Brigantes' rights or the Romans'? Is either reason enough to take a man's life—or for a man to give it? Dead is dead, and you've neither freedom *nor* civilization, if you're six feet under. Do it for posterity, you say? Has posterity ever learned a lesson from the past? Was there ever a war that ended all wars? Is it worth laying down one's life for posterity when posterity ups and takes away the freedom of someone else? Is there never a point at which man will say that war is obsolete? Somewhere there must be superior beings. I don't think I could bear to believe that man—here on this earth—is the epitome of the highest intelligence in the universe.

"The past is important to me because it is the only way we can plan the future. If we don't learn from it, we're doomed to go on repeating the same mistakes. Sometimes, when I touch a stone on the wall placed there by a Roman legionary, I wonder if he knew that, almost two-thousand years later, someone would come to that very spot and wonder about it. I used to wish that I could have been a part of it all —the ships, the building, the making of a city. Perhaps I could have redirected its course, prevented some of its brutalities. And maybe, because I once wished it so, the past has come to me."

"And you're sorry now?"

"How do I know until the scene ends? But each time the soldiers return, the dread deepens. I doubt very much that there's a happy ending."

A fringe of light was creeping up on the horizon. For a moment Dan feared a return of the soldiers, but then he recognized the first gray streaks of dawn. Had the chase and the fight lasted all night, then? Or had the hours passed as they were talking? It was morning already, and he would be leaving for London that afternoon.

It was not the past Dan wished he could change, it was the future. If he could have an effect on anything, he'd like to bring about a world with no nuclear weapons, no Huntington's disease, no dying till you'd reached the grand old age of ninety and had an illustrious career to remember. And yet . . . ?

"I'm tied to the past whether I like it or not because of heredity," he told Joe. "I'd like to hope that maybe I'll be the one to break the chain, and that Huntington's disease will be wiped out forever in our line. But of course it will be a long time before I know."

Joe nodded. "We're all drawn to the past for different reasons. For Ambrose, traditions are important because they make one's position in a clan secure. He knows what is expected of him and his children because it has always been so. He looks to the past for guidelines, for rules about the way he should live his life. The more unrewarding the present, the more uncertain the future, the more he turns to the past. For Ambrose there have been too many changes, too fast. The Romany ways are slipping off. Jasper is not really fit to take over when Ambrose is gone; Nat has little taste for the Traveler's life; there is always the possibility that Orlenda will run off with a *gorgio*. Ambrose's pleasure comes not from anticipating what lies ahead, but in reveling in what went before."

"And Jasper?"

"Who knows? Perhaps Ambrose tried too hard to make him a good Romany. He was too harsh, too strict, too demanding. . . . Perhaps this is Jasper's way of backing out. No one expects things of a mute, you see. There is nothing for him to live up to, and he can go his own way. Perhaps he is smarter than any of us realize. Sometimes I think that only the old granny understood him; and what powers he has, he got from her."

"Have you ever told the Faws about the soldiers?"

"No, nor is it something I will ever do. Ghosts are considered a frightful omen among the Romanies."

"But they know that Jasper sees things, hears things. . . ."

"Aye, but they don't know what, do they?"

"Don't they ever hear the singing?"

"Probably, but they don't talk about things they don't understand."

"Then there are many things you can never discuss with Ambrose."

"It's true. There is always a distance between us. Respect more than friendship."

In the early morning darkness, Dan could see shadowy figures coming up the hill toward the grave, a group outnumbering the Faws. He stood up stiffly, conscious of the bruises on his legs.

"The Boswells have come, then," Joe said.

Strangely, Ambrose did not question the presence of Joe and Dan on the hilltop. He led the second gypsy clan over to the grave where the ceremony of the day before was repeated: the Romany prayers, the weeping, and the placing of heather upon the freshly dug plot. In the fog of early morning, the women's dresses were muted blurs of red, yellow, and purple, while the men stood off to one side in grays and browns, arms hanging loosely, hands clasped in front, heads bowed.

"Dan. . . ."

Dan look around. Nat was standing there shoeless, his eyes still creased with sleep, his shirt not quite tucked in his pants.

"Come here," he whispered.

"Where?"

"Down here."

Dan turned and followed the boy back to camp. Already a meal of potatoes and beans was cooking on the fire. Orlenda squatted beside it, feeding in sticks one at a time, the flames licking at her fingers. She followed Dan with her eyes but did not speak.

"Come in here," said Nat, going up the steps of the *vardo*.

"I can't go in there," Dan protested, but Nat motioned impatiently. "Come *on!*"

A small kerosene lamp burned on the wall above the chest of drawers on the right. On the left side of the *vardo* stood a stove, a closet, and at the very back, beneath a high window, a thickly blanketed bed built off the floor above a cupboard. The doors of the cupboard were open, revealing a smaller bed where Rachel was still sleeping.

It was an old wagon, and the walls and ceilings, richly sculptured with intertwining grape leaves, were faded, the paint chipping. The brass angel on the stem of the wall lamp was tarnished and dull. The whole had the smell of age—the well-scrubbed wood, the polish, the wax that had yellowed, the worn carpet on the floor, the grease on the stove. . . .

Again Dan felt the impropriety of his presence there.

"What do you want, Nat?"

"You said you'd trade your belt and boots this morning. . . ."

"I didn't say my boots."

"Please, your boots, too."

"No, only my belt." As soon as he'd said it, Dan knew he'd been taken. He smiled at his own naiveté. "Okay, what will you give me for it?"

Nat opened a drawer in the bureau and took out a buck knife. Dan shook his head.

"I've got one. No deal."

Rachel lifted her head from the pillow without opening her eyes, stretched her neck and arms, and then curled up again. Nat continued to rummage about in the drawer and finally handed Dan a compass, doubtless an antique. Dan was tempted.

He looked it over, turning it slightly, but the needle turned with it. "Come on, Nat. This thing doesn't even work. I thought you said you had something to trade!" He made a pretense of turning to leave. He'd show Nat that he couldn't trick a *gorgio*—he wouldn't have them all laughing at him after he left.

"Wait a minute."

Nat was digging down in his pocket. He paused a moment, as though wrestling with the decision, then quickly took out a coin. "Here."

"What is it?" Dan took it over to the lamp and examined it closely.

It was a small Roman silver piece, about the size of a penny. On one side was a portrait of the emperor wearing a laurel wreath and the inscription IMP. CASER, VESPESIANVS. AVG. On the other side was Neptune, bearded and muscular, with one foot on the prow of a ship, a dolphin in one hand and trident in the other, and a second inscription: COS. OTER. TR. POT.

"This is yours?" Dan questioned.

The boy nodded.

"Where'd you get it?"

Nat shrugged. "They're around." He watched Dan earnestly.

Dan felt as Joe Stanton had said he'd felt, cupping his hand over a stone that a Roman soldier had laid. Who knew how many hands from ages past had held this coin, what it had purchased, what debts it had paid?

"Okay," he said, deciding not to drag the trading out any longer. He put the coin in his pocket and took off his belt. Nat smiled broadly, admired the buckle, and turned it over and over in his hands before tucking it away in the drawer.

Dan went back outside and over to Orlenda, who still sat hunched by the fire. Occasionally she reached up and stirred the pot that hung on a black smoky hook.

He felt overcome suddenly with exhaustion, remembering that he had not slept. He sat down beside her and helped feed the sticks into the fire, slowly, so that the flames burned just so high around the pot and no higher. He noticed her looking at him out of the corner of her eye and was conscious of his own grimy, unkempt appearance. It must have seemed highly disrespectful to the dead.

"I'm sorry," he apologized. "I didn't sleep at all last night. Something happened."

She looked quickly at him, then just as quickly turned away. Some of the Boswell children had come back down the hill to the camp, and Nat went over to them. Orlenda sent them all to the stream with buckets for water.

"Were you awake last night?" Dan asked, continuing the conversation. "Did you hear them?"

"I wasn't awake," she said.

"But did you hear them?" he asked again. "The Roman soldiers?"

She stared at him, then quickly shook her head as though to quiet him. "If you speak of such things, they come back."

Dan waited. She would talk to him about it, he was sure of it. He had to know what others had seen, what others had heard—had to make sense of things before he left.

"I saw them," he said finally. "One tried to catch me, and we wrestled. That's why. . . ." He held out his arms to show her the dirt on his shirt, watching her face, but she showed no expression at all.

Again the silence.

"Do you believe in ghosts, Orlenda?"

"Of course. They're all about."

"But you've never seen them?"

She turned her back, as though to end the conversation. But Dan did not move away, so she said finally, "If I *were* to see one, it would be that of my grandmother, because I have a special feeling for her. Some see things of the past, some of the future. But I have seen nothing."

"Neither did I, before I came to York." He stirred the pot for her. "Who else has seen them besides me?"

She hesistated. Then, "Jasper. And Granny. Granny used to see a magpie. She would go down to the creek to wash clothes, and she'd come back and say, 'It was the magpie I saw today that will cry at my wake.' She would see things in the water, you know. It is always the water they come from. And it was always the future with Granny. Well, the magpie came, but it didn't cry. It made no sound at all. And Mother's been worried. One magpie without a mate is always bad luck. But a magpie at a funeral, well. . . ." She poked quickly at the fire as though it would stop her from saying any more.

"And no one else has seen anything? Ambrose? Your mother? Nat?"

She laughed then. "Never Nat. Nat feels nothing for the Romanies. He will leave to be a *gorgio*. Mother has already predicted it. Granny knew it before he was born. Already he talks of leaving us."

146

From far off on the hill, the gypsies were returning. He and Joe would be leaving soon, and it was
Dan's last chance to ask the question that had been
bothering him the most. He would risk it.

"What does your mother know about me, Orlenda?"

"What do you mean?"

"What did she see in my palm that day? Did she
ever tell you?"

Orlenda stood up suddenly and shook out her
apron. "Mother is wrong sometimes," she said.

"But what did she see?" Dan pleaded.

Orlenda, however, moved away, and Ambrose
came between them, warming his hands at the fire.

THE GRANDMOTHER'S BED OF BRACKEN, all of her
dishes, her clothes, her slippers, her gilded chest—
everything under the tarp—was saturated with
melted paraffin. While the company of Boswells
stood by, Rose carried a burning stick from the fire to
the death tent and set it aflame.

Like a river of molten lava, the long spiraling
thread of paraffin ignited, a zigzag of lightning under
the canvas. The abandoned possessions of the old
woman went up in a roar, like a wind blowing across
England from the west, from across the Irish sea.

Rose wept, and Orlenda circled her with her slim
brown arms, dark head on her mother's shoulder.

"They'll see it now, the *gavvers*," one of the Boswells said.

"We'll eat together, then, and meet in Pickering,"

Ambrose told them. "The *gavvers* won't interrupt a funeral meal. At least we'll have potatoes in our stomachs before we start."

"Aye," said the second man. "In Pickering, then. There's a chap with a pony to trade that I'll give two horses for and get one, but I'll have the best of the bargain."

Joe and Dan ate one helping of beans and potatoes, then took their leave of the Faws.

"The lad's parents will be expecting him back, so it's best we get on," Joe explained. "Good luck and good health, Ambrose. I'll have need of you when you're back this way again."

Ambrose nodded, grasped Joe's hand, clutched his shoulder with the other hand in a silent gesture of farewell. He did the same to Dan, but Jasper backed off when Dan turned to him. There was something about his eyes at that moment that seemed so threatening, yet fearful; hostile, yet confused, that it looked as though he were on the verge of crying out, of saying something. But then, as Dan hesitated—waiting—he turned quickly and fled off among the trees.

The Boswells were talking in Romany among themselves and felt no obligation to do more than nod in the direction of the parting guests. Nat, sitting on top the *vardo* with his plate of beans, gave Dan a fancy salute and winked. Rose's departing gesture was perhaps the warmest.

She came over to Dan, grasped his arm tightly

with both her hands, and said, "Have a safe trip back to America, Dan, and come to see us again."

"When I'm thirty-five?" Dan asked, watching her carefully. "Will I still be able to travel then?"

She smiled good-naturedly. "Only fools want to know the future, Dan. Do not ask it. When you feed tomorrow, it eats the joy of today."

It was like something out of a Chinese fortune cookie, Dan decided. Were they believers or were they charlatans?

Only Orlenda was left. She would not, he knew, ever say goodbye, for gypsies feel it to be bad luck to wish a goodbye on anyone. Yet she did not even look at Dan as he got in the cab and Joe turned it around in the clearing. She stood with her back against the *vardo*, her eyes on the sky. As they started down the deeply rutted path to the lane, however, she sprang forward suddenly and pointed to a bird sitting high on a branch ahead of them.

The magpie.

8

THEY WERE ALMOST like strangers on the road back to York. Several times Joe drummed his fingers on the steering wheel and shifted slightly as if he were on the verge of words, but words did not come. It was as though any remark now would be so trite, after their experience, as to be meaningless.

It was raining. The wipers made a knocking noise as they arrived dead center, then sprang apart in silence and collided again.

"They won't be offended that we left so soon?" Dan asked finally.

"No. This meal should rightly belong to the clans. They'll speak Romany if we're not there and enjoy it the more."

Another long stretch of silence, broken only by the noise of the wipers.

"Your mum and dad will be back early this afternoon, do you think?" Joe asked finally.

The tightness in the chest again, the cold, the dread . . .

"You think they'll follow me, then?"

"Perhaps when you leave the country that will be the end of it."

Joe drove the cab through Monk Bar and headed south on Goodramgate. "But what was Ambrose doing in the Tower?"

"Hiding from the police."

"Eh?"

"He'd gone to get the sod for the coffin—from the place where the old grandmother had been born down at the end of the garden. The police were making their rounds, and so he hid in the Tower."

Joe sat rigidly behind the wheel. "He wouldn't have hid in the Tower. He wouldn't corner himself like that."

The fear seemed to leap up and clutch at Dan's throat.

"How do you know, Joe? Maybe it just seemed like the best thing to do at the time."

"The old woman wasn't even born in York, she was born in Aldborough. She told me once herself."

Dan felt sick at his stomach and overcome, suddenly, with exhaustion. He was angry, embarrassed at his gullibility, tired of this senseless charade, which was beyond reason or understanding. He felt certain now that the gypsies had anticipated his visit long before he had come, and had been waiting for him.

Whether Joe was involved or not, he didn't know. But he was too tired to be on the outs with Joe. He needed to trust someone.

"What would Ambrose have been doing in the Tower then, in the rain, at that time of night?" he asked, his voice weak and thin. "And there *was* a piece of sod on the grandmother's chest."

"Only Ambrose could tell you what it all meant, Dan, and he obviously didn't tell you the truth."

The cab came to a stop in front of the hotel. They sat for a few moments, watching the rain streaming down the windshield. It seemed the wrong time to be taking leave of each other, as if each would need the other's support sometime again.

"Well," Dan said at last, "it's hard to say goodbye, Joe. You've been great. And what's happened—it's nothing you could help. I appreciate your taking me around like you did."

Joe reached over, grabbed his hand, held it a moment, and let go.

As Dan opened the door and stepped out, he almost bumped into Mrs. Harrison, who was coming up the sidewalk under a large umbrella. She stopped and stared at his clothes.

"Well, now, what's 'appened to you, eh?" she said, peering at him through the rain. "It's as though e's slept in a pig sty, Mr. Stanton!"

"A bit of a problem with the cab, Mrs. Harrison," Joe called out. "Dan gave me a hand, and he's the worse for it, I'm afraid."

"Take a hot tub, lad, and I'll send tea up," the woman said, going on inside.

Dan bent over and gave Joe a quick salute.

"Take care," Joe said, looking at him intently, and then the cab drove on.

It was only as Dan started up the steps that he remembered the coin in his pocket. He'd meant to ask Joe about it, find out what it was and how much it was worth, but the cab had already reached the corner and was turning away.

HE SLEPT LIKE THE DEAD, having bathed in the big English tub for the last time and fallen exhausted into bed. It was a dreamless sleep, with no fears, no fantasies—nothing but unconsciousness. He did not waken till his parents came in about one.

"Dan, I thought you'd be packed by now!" Mrs. Roberts said. "Do you realize the day's half over?" She opened the drapes. "We had such a marvelous time in Scarborough. You really would have loved it! We've just got to come back to England."

Dan slowly opened his eyes and closed them again. It seemed as though it had never happened, as though the deep sleep had erased all dread, all confusion. It was as if now that he was leaving York the town had released its hold on him.

He tried to keep his eyes open and focused on his father standing in the doorway, laughing at him. "Joe must have taken you out on the town last night," he kidded. "Think you can sit up, old boy?"

Dan smiled and managed to get both legs over the side of the bed. He sleepily watched his mother rummaging about through the clothes he had thrown on the floor.

"Oh, Dan, look at this shirt! It's filthy!"

"I know. I was outdoors most of the time—had to rough it."

"And your jeans, Dan! These are the only decent pants you've got left to wear. They're so wrinkled!"

Mr. Roberts came on into the room. "Nobody's going to notice, Ruth. How did things go while we were gone, Dan? Glad you stayed behind?"

"Yeah. Fantastic. Take me a year to tell you all about it."

"Well, right now you've simply got to get up and start packing," his mother said. "Mrs. Harrison said she'd find someone to drive us to the station."

Later, while she made a final check of their rooms and Dan's father settled their account at the desk, Dan walked back to Micklegate Bar for the last time. The rain had slowed to a drizzle, and he wanted to go up on the wall and look out over the whole city —to imprint the place on his mind. He wanted to be able to close his eyes and remember it exactly.

Why had he felt such apprehension at this small north country town, this mere dot on the map of Britain, this microscopic moment in the history of civilization? What had terrified him so about the Multangular Tower or the cellar of the Treasurer's House? Why could he think about them now with none of that dread whatsoever? Why did it seem as though the incident at the camp last night had never happened, and that the soldiers had never come? A good sleep, was that all he had needed? Had his mind been as fatigued as all that?

Fatigue, excitement, worry, the surroundings— they had all made him prone to hallucinations. That and, possibly the drink that the Faws had served. A prime target for self-hypnosis, that's what he was. Gullible. Oversensitive. Not the best qualities for a journalist. He'd have to work on that.

Still, his own hallucinations didn't explain Joe Stanton's.

He stood across from Micklegate Bar and viewed it through the mist—objectively, as any tourist might see it. There were the towers, the banners, the three statues on top, the narrow crosslike windows. . . . Interesting. Quaint.

He went on up the steps to the wall and quickly scanned the city—the rooftops, the spires, the flowers, the tangle of streets and the serpentine wall. . . . This is the way he would remember it, full of historic charm, nothing more. Good. He was done with it now, and the spell was broken.

He went back down the steps and along the street toward the hotel. As he did so, he thrust his hands into his pockets and instantly felt the coin. He stopped and slowly took it out, holding it in the palm of his hand. It was bitterly cold, like ice boring through his skin.

And suddenly he realized it was not the coin that was cold, but his hand; and a moment later the dread —the awful, sweeping sensation of terror—was upon him once more. He sucked in his breath and turned toward Micklegate Bar for reassurance, to capture the bravado he had felt only a moment before. It was no longer the tall paternal landmark he had known, however, for the wall on either side had become alive with shadows—tall and short, bobbing up and down as though announcing the approach of horsemen. The gate itself was transformed into a living thing, the narrow slits of windows becoming eyes and the gaping arch beneath a huge mouth, which shrieked after him as he fled.

He ran back to the inn, breathing loudly, letting sound escape from his lips to help release the panic. The only solution was to leave York forever. He would have the coin appraised when he got home and sell it. So much for antiquity. He was disgusted with himself, yet the dread remained like an icy fist in the pit of the stomach.

By the time they were on the train, the rain had begun again in earnest. It streamed down the coach windows, making watery images of the trees beyond. Dan sat facing his parents across a small table. Other passengers were eating the home-packed suppers they had brought with them, or sitting primly behind the pages of the *Manchester Guardian*, ignoring the smells of sausage rolls and cheese.

158

"I can't believe we'll be home tomorrow," Mrs. Roberts said, trying to see through the window and finally giving up. "Oh, I hope the storm breaks before we reach London! Our last night there—I'd hate for it to be ruined."

"Not going to let a little rain spoil it, are you?" said Dan's father, putting one arm about her. "Come on Ruth, show the proper British spirit."

It was warm and friendly there in the coach, with the laughter of some young men from Aberdeen in the compartment who were involved in a fast-moving card game. The dread had subsided again, and Dan felt comfortable, if not entirely in control of his feelings. Once they reached London, and surely once they were home, he decided, the dread would disappear completely. Give him forty-eight hours of American food and two nights on his own mattress, and he would see the events of the last eleven days for what they were: a time warp in the brain, a short-circuit brought on by fatigue and gypsies and the superstitions of an addled cab driver. He was not quite sure enough of his feelings to risk taking out the coin again, but that would come later.

He wanted to say something to his parents, however, that would be comforting. He wanted to sum up the trip, somehow, and let them know he appreciated it. He longed to do even more: to make them hopeful, especially his father. He wanted them always to be as they were just then—jovial and laughing, enjoying something together. . . .

"You're right, Dad," he said. "We won't let a little rain spoil our last night in London. We can't make up our minds in advance about the way things have to be."

It did not come out as profound as he had hoped.

"What I mean is, we can get so uptight about what might or might not happen that we let it ruin what we've got going for us right now."

Rose Faw's words came instantly to mind: *Feed tomorrow and it will eat the joy of today.* He repeated it to his parents.

"Isn't that just like a gypsy?" Mother said. "There's something to be said for a philosophy like that—no worry, no planning. . . . They probably live to a ripe old age."

"So that's the way we'll live." Mr. Roberts' warm smile embraced them both. "What will be will be. We're not going to live the next ten or twenty years thinking 'what if?' You may have to remind me of that now and then, but as you said, let's not ruin what we've got right now."

The assurances given, the bonds strengthened, they each settled back with their own private thoughts while rivulets of water streamed down the window, collecting in a small river at the bottom of the glass.

It was a comfort being there with each other, a comfort to know that they were all in it together. The laughter of the men brought smiles to their own lips, and Dan stretched out his legs and leaned back.

A baby, passing by in the aisle, looked over her mother's shoulder, her dark eyes staring unabashedly at Dan, face sober. The eyes reminded Dan of Rachel. Then it was Orlenda's eyes he remembered.

Why had she said nothing to him when he left? Was she hoping, somehow, that she might see him again? And why had she pointed out the magpie just above him? A warning?

It was not true about gypsies being carefree, never thinking of tomorrow. All of the rituals, the superstitions—the burning of the death tent, the thornbush on the grave, the magpie, the bloodless killing of the chickens—weren't they all linked to a yearning to have some control over their own destiny? If you put aside traveling for a day because a magpie flew into your circle, wasn't that worry about what would happen the day after or the next or the next?

Was there anyone, in any age, who had never been apprehensive about the future? Wasn't that one of the things that distinguished man from the animals: the ability—or the curse perhaps—to worry? As long as a dog had food in its stomach, did it care about where the next meal was coming from? As long as its master was about, did it worry about whether he might go away?

Dan's mind played with the ideas, back and forth. Part of his feature story, maybe? A concluding paragraph on life and chance? Bill would appreciate that, would like the deductions. Original. Thoughtful. He'd work it up on the plane going home.

Then he thought of Nat again, the way he sat up there on the bow-topped *vardo,* one leg dangling down each side, holding his tin dinner plate and winking slyly at Dan. By now the Faws and the Boswells together would be on their way to Pickering. The *gavvers* would have seen the smoke of the burning and come by. Or perhaps the farmer himself would have smelled the acrid odor of charred canvas and hiked down over the field to investigate. One way or the other, they'd be driven off, not that they weren't about to leave anyway.

The *vardos* would be moving in a small procession, the big draft horse pulling the Faws' wagon. Rose and Rachel would ride inside, and Orlenda would ride in the smaller cart, pulled by a second horse. The piebald pony would take the lead, no doubt, with Nat on its back, whistling, swaggering, showing off to the Boswell kids, and wearing Dan's belt, which was still inches too big for him.

Dan smiled. Nat would lie, of course. He'd tell them he had made a fantastic trade—that he had given Dan something worthless in its place. The memory of the coin brought only a vague uneasiness, and Dan found that he could dismiss it easily by concentrating on the caravan as Joe had described it— the dogs running in the ditch along the road, bursting through the hedge now and then after a hare or a badger; the men, Ambrose and Jasper, walking along beside, and the squeak of the wheels would be rhythmical, hypnotic. . . .

Old Ambrose—what had he been up to that night in the Tower? To no good, that was certain.

Dan wished that his last ride home with Joe Stanton had not been quite so tense and upsetting—that he had not told him about going to the Tower. It would only make him worry. Perhaps he would write to Joe after he got back to the States. Genteel Joe—he was as superstitious as the rest, for all his books and reading, his lectures and tours. Joe had lived in York too long. He had embalmed himself in its antiquity.

I'm glad I'm getting out, Dan thought. It was time to see Bill again, to work on the newspaper, to immerse himself in the present and get his head on straight. Tomorrow—home.

THE RAIN CAME DOWN in York as well. Despite the deluge, a swarthy man in old trousers and a jacket that did not match came riding down from the north road on a piebald pony.

The animal had its head turned away from the wind, its long shaggy hair clinging to its body, damp and bedraggled, a cloud of steam rising from its nostrils, its sides heaving. Clumps of mud flew out from behind its hooves, and it snorted with displeasure when the rider dug his heels into its flanks.

When they reached the small hotel, the pony was tied to a lamp post, and it whinnied and stomped. But then, after a word from the gypsy, it stood quietly with its head down, resigned to the weather.

The porters, standing inside the door, watched and whispered together, then turned and called out something to someone behind the desk. When Ambrose Faw burst through the doors of the hotel, his jacket soaked, his boots squeaking, Mrs. Harrison, forewarned, stood like an immovable fortress at her post, hands resting on the counter, as though defending the establishment with her very body.

"Yes?"

"Pardon, Missus, but I'm looking for the American boy."

She stared at him. "Dan? Dan Roberts?"

Ambrose nodded.

" 'e's not 'ere. Left with 'is parents an hour ago for London."

Ambrose stood motionless, unblinking, the water running down over his eyelids from his hair. The porters gathered in the hallway off to the left, staring.

"He's gone, then?"

"I told you, didn't I? An hour ago."

The bearded man did not move. Mrs. Harrison raised her eyebrows and looked over at the bell captain, who was fidgeting uneasily. Then Ambrose spoke again.

"Did he happen to . . . to leave a coin at the desk, Missus?"

"Well *I* don't know!" Mrs. Harrison's voice rose in exasperation, and her lips formed the familiar "O." "Might be 'e wanted change for the sweets machines or something. I don't stand 'ere all day at the desk, mind you!"

"It was a special coin . . . a piece of Roman silver."

"Well, a smart chap like 'im wouldn't go about puttin' Roman coins in sweets machines, then, would 'e? Like as not 'e's taken it with him—a souvenir, don't you know?"

Ambrose whirled about, spraying water off his head, his beard, droplets falling on the registry book.

"Look 'ere, now!" Mrs. Harrison cried, dabbing at the blurred ink with her handkerchief, but Ambrose bolted out the door and leaped on the pony.

Clattering down the street, he charged through Micklegate Bar with neither a look to the right nor left, past Priory Street and Trinity Lane and on toward the River. There he urged the pony down the bank until it was standing in water halfway up its flanks.

Unloosening Dan's belt, which he had buckled onto his own, Ambrose flung it as far out into the water as it would go, howling an oath to the heavens, baying like a wolf.

The current grasped at the belt, the buckle dragging, swallowed it up, and continued its eternal rush down the Ouse to the Humber, and on at last to the sea.

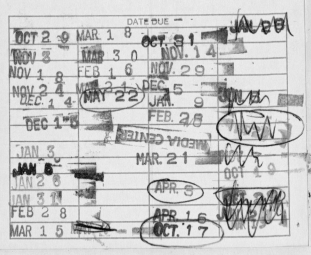

DATE DUE

OCT 2 9	MAR. 1 8	OCT. 3 1	JAN 22
NOV 3	MAR 3 0	NOV. 1 4	
NOV 1 8	FEB 1 6	NOV. 29	
NOV 2 4	MAY 2 4	DEC. 5	
DEC. 1 4	MAY 22	JAN. 9	JUN 14
DEC 1 8		FEB. 28	
JAN 3	MEDIA CENTER	MAR. 21	
JAN 6			OCT 1 9
JAN 2 6		APR. 9	
JAN 3 1			
FEB 2 8		APR. 1 6	
MAR 1 5		OCT. 1 7	

6146

MAR 13

APR 24

FIC
NAY

Naylor, Phyllis
Reynolds.

Shadows on the wall.

17192

312140 01462D